The Album of Dr. Moreau

THE ALBUM OF DR. MOREAU

DARYL GREGORY

TOR
DOT
COM

A TOM DOHERTY ASSOCIATES BOOK

NEW YORK

THE ALBUM OF DR. MOREAU

Cover design by FORT

Edited by Jonathan Strahan

A Tordotcom Book
Published by Tom Doherty Associates
120 Broadway
New York, NY 10271

www.tor.com

Tor® is a registered trademark of Macmillan Publishing Group, LLC.

ISBN 978-1-250-78211-3 (ebook)
ISBN 978-1-250-78210-6 (trade paperback)

First Edition: May 2021

The Album of Dr. Moreau

T. S. Eliot's Five Rules of Detective Fiction

1. The story must not rely upon elaborate and incredible disguises.
2. The character and motives of the criminal should be normal . . . if the criminal is highly abnormal an irrational element is introduced which offends us.
3. The story must not rely either upon occult phenomena, or, what comes to the same thing, upon mysterious and preposterous discoveries made by lonely scientists. . . . Writers of this sort of hocus-pocus may think that they are fortified by the prestige of H. G. Wells. But observe that Wells triumphs with his scientific fiction just because he keeps within the limits of a genre which is different from the detective genre. The reality is on another plane. In detective fiction there is no place for this sort of thing.
4. Elaborate and bizarre machinery is an irrelevance.
5. The detective should be highly intelligent but not super-human. We should be able to follow his inferences and almost, but not quite, make them with him.

—From "Homage to Wilkie Collins: An Omnibus Review of Nine Mystery Novels" by T. S. Eliot, writing in *New Criterion*, January 1927

Intro

MAY 18, 2021
5°03′43.2″S 101°31′19.7″W

Dear Melanie,

I hope this letter finds you well. In fact, I hope it finds you at all. I've sent it to your manager, and I fear it might get lost in the volumes of fan mail you must receive. Back in the WyldBoyZ heyday we needed a small team of assistants to sort the mail into Ignore, Reply, and Report to Police. These days, I suppose, your fan mail comes by email or Twitter or whatever social media platform is the hot new thing. (Forgive me, that makes me sound as old as I am.)

I've followed your career as closely as I followed your mother's—closer, if I'm honest. I suppose that's understandable—professional interest and all that. Your songs are beautiful, Melanie. I can hardly believe that you're not yet thirty and yet you've accomplished so much. But I shouldn't be surprised. We only met that one night, but you were a lovely, talented girl then, and you grew up with a lovely, fierce mother as a role model. (Every pop star needs a fierce mother to either lean on or rebel against.)

Speaking of your mother, please pass on my congratulations on her well-deserved retirement. So many bad guys put behind bars! I hope that her reputation was not too damaged by the fact that the killer in her most famous case was never apprehended. She should take this opportunity to travel. Or do some reading. Or both. . . .

Which brings us to my retirement gift. It's nothing, really—a harmless bit of science fiction from a bygone era, like the H. G. Wells novel Dr. M stole his name from, or O. J. Simpson's If I Did It. I hope she enjoys it.

I've enclosed a gift for you, as well. Though your own work ranges across the musical spectrum—I can hear traces of everything from Édith Piaf to Prince to Konono Nº1—I hope that deep down (deep down, deep down) you keep a place in your heart for the WyldBoyZ. I also hope you have a CD player.

—A Fan

Track 1

"Wakin' Up (Next to U)"

Featuring Bobby O

The penthouse rooms were decorated in a midwestern car salesman's idea of how rich people live: glass, chrome, mirrors, enough marble to bury a small village, track lights bouncing off every surface. Call it Modern American Lens Flare.

Of course, by the time the Director of Housekeeping—her name was Ana Gomez, if I recall correctly (and I do)—keyed in that morning, the suite had been trashed. The party had left in its wake a miniature forest of champagne glasses and Zima bottles, trays of warm salami, savaged cheese wheels, a gigantic glass bowl where headless, desultory shrimp soaked in a dirty pink bath. White drapes billowed in front of an open balcony door, the lace speckled with what looked at first glance to be drops of Cabernet.

Gomez surveyed the damage. She was a twenty-year veteran of the hospitality industry—Las Vegas hospitality, a special circle of hell—and had seen worse. She walked slowly down the long hallway, singing out the traditional warning cry of her guild: "Housekeeping!" The Jacuzzi sat empty, surrounded by a scattering of damp underwear as thin and transparent as dying jellyfish. The first guest bedroom was ransacked but empty, as was the second. In the theater room, the screen displayed a brilliant, dead blue.

Then Gomez reached the master bedroom. "Housekeeping," she said again.

A tawny arm protruded from the silken sheets. A long, clawed hand twitched. Ms. Gomez of course knew who had rented the penthouse, as well as all of the rooms on this floor. The WyldBoyZ had performed the previous night at the Matador Grand Arena. The band's fans—the ones old enough to own a credit card, anyway—had bought up the hotel's rooms and filled the bars and restaurants. You could tell them by their animal costumes: furry tails, cat ears, prosthetic tusks, bat wings. An alarming number wore head-to-toe outfits like sports mascots.

But this arm, this was no costume. Gomez hadn't seen one of these "hybrids" up close, and her first thought—this is in the trial transcripts—was the same thought everyone had, when they first met one of the boyz: "He looked so *realistic*."

Then she realized the arm was covered in realistic blood.

Gomez didn't scream. She was a pro.

The owner of the arm sat up. Blinked. Rubbed his whiskers, which smeared a little blood across his cheeks. Yawned (adorably).

That's when Gomez screamed.

Bobby O, the youngest and most feline member of the band, was covered in blood from his neck to the waistband of his tighty-whities. The rest of his body remained under the covers.

Bobby raised a hand/paw. As with many of the boyz' anatomical features, the definition of the category was blurry:

Each hand possessed a humanlike thumb, but his fingers were short, and furred. His claws weren't extended at that moment, but when they were out they added another three inches to each finger.

"Hi," he said. Smiled bashfully. Ana Gomez, Director of Housekeeping, ran from the room.

––––––––

Bobby stood up, feeling wobbly and hungover. Whose room was he in? What city was this? They'd been on the road so long he wasn't worried when answers didn't immediately come to mind. Though he did wonder why that woman had freaked out.

Then he caught a glimpse of himself in a wall of mirrors. Looked down at his chest. And said, "Oh. Shit."

Blood had smeared not only his chest and underwear but also his legs and feet. He looked like he'd rolled in it. He swiped his chest and sniffed his hand.

Was he dying? He wasn't sure. It was true that he didn't feel *great*. He'd remembered drinking the usual amount of Red Bull and Smirnoff last night and snorting perhaps a smidge more than the usual amount of cocaine, because . . . that's right! It was the last night of the tour. But this, this was the worst hangover of his life. His entire body ached, as if he'd been steamrollered flat and partially re-inflated, Tom and Jerry style. Which was a terrible feeling, but not, like, hemorrhaging-from-multiple-gunshot-wounds bad. In fact, there didn't seem to be a wound visible. Also, the blood didn't smell like his.

He touched his tongue to his hand. Nope, didn't taste like his, either.

He twisted to look at his back in the mirror and saw the mound under the sheets. He'd been sleeping beside that lump since, well, sometime during his blackout. He crept toward the California king bed and reached toward the bedcover. "Please don't be a dead hooker," he murmured. "Please don't be a dead hooker. . . ."

He peeled back the sheet. Leapt back with a yowl. "Why couldn't it be a dead hooker?!"

He bolted from the bedroom. It was slowly coming back to him where he was and, more important, where he should be, which was: Not Here.

The corridor was empty, thank God. Gomez and the maids had fled, leaving behind their carts. Bobby's room was to the . . . left? Yes. And Tusk's room was across from Bobby's.

He banged on Tusk's door and kept banging until it opened.

Tusk filled the doorway. He was six years older than Bobby O and four times his size: six-foot-seven, 450 pounds (give or take), arms and legs as thick as you'd expect from a person whose DNA contained a significant amount of pachyderm. He was sensitive about his size, perhaps a side effect of being under constant scrutiny by the Teen Idol Industrial Complex. He wore his favorite Aloha-print pajamas, green silk kimono, and reinforced pink bunny slippers, all custom-made.

"Oh my goodness, Bobby," Tusk said. His voice was surprisingly high for such a big boy. "What did you do?"

Bobby pointed back the way he'd come. "Dr. M!"

Tusk leaned out into the hallway. Bloody paw prints led down the carpet, ending at Bobby's furry feet. The trouble had been brought straight to Tusk's door.

"You gotta come!" Bobby said.

"Do I?" Tusk asked.

A door opened in the opposite direction, twenty feet away. Matt stepped out. As usual, he was wearing one of his fringed ponchos, pretty much the only fashion option available to a giant bat. "Would you guys keep it down? It's not even noon." With one hand he lifted the headphones from his triangle ears and let them drop around his neck.

"Bobby wants us to go to Dr. M's room," Tusk said.

"He's dead!" Bobby exclaimed.

"What? Are you sure?" Tusk asked.

"Literally!" Bobby had recently learned what the word literally meant.

"That *is* a lot of blood he's wearing," Matt said.

The three of them hurried to the suite, avoiding stepping on the bloody prints, and stopped in front of the door, which was still ajar. Tusk nodded to the supply carts. "Are there maids in there?"

Bobby told them about waking up in Dr. M's bed, the woman in the suite screaming at him, and then seeing the body for himself. "Come on, I'll show you." He reached for the doorknob and Tusk stopped him, handed him a towel from the cart.

"You'd better wipe off," Tusk said.

"And stop touching things," Matt said.

"You stop touching things," Bobby said.

"Guys!" Tusk pushed the door open with his elbow and walked to the master bedroom.

Dr. M, born Maurice Bendix, filled much of the bed. He was a big man, a size Matt referred to as Late Stage Brando.

The body had been gouged apart. Deep, raking wounds parted the flesh from neck to groin. Blood had soaked into the bed, forming a dark red paste.

"Doc?" Tusk asked quietly.

"Really?" Matt said. "You think he'll answer?"

Dr. M's mouth was agape, and his eyes were wide, staring at the ceiling. They all looked up. The ceiling was mirrored, of course. Somehow this more than doubled the gruesomeness of the scene.

"I didn't do it," Bobby said.

Matt said, "You better hope you don't have any deep tissue under your nails."

"I didn't touch him!"

"No, you just crawled in bed with him. And then somehow slept through the part where he got carved into chunks beside you."

"No! I mean, I don't . . ." Bobby's ears were pinned back in fear. "I don't remember."

"How did you even get in here?" Tusk asked. "I locked you in your room last night. I sat in the hallway, blocking the doorway, because you were in Maximum Bob Mode."

Bobby had the decency to look embarrassed. "That checks out."

"So?" Tusk asked. "Any guesses?"

"I think I climbed."

"What?"

"I kinda remember climbing out on the balcony and then . . . jumping?"

Matt shook his head. "Dude, we're fifty-seven stories up."

Tusk's big hand rubbed his gray temple. "Why couldn't you stay in your room, Bobby?" But he knew why; they all did. When Bobby was in Maximum Bob Mode, too much was never enough. Dr. M's suite contained all the drink and all the drugs, and of course he'd try to get back there, even blackout drunk. Tusk hadn't imagined, however, that Bobby would be maximized enough to leap from balcony to balcony.

"Did you see anybody else here?" Tusk asked.

Bobby shook his head.

"Are you sure? I saw a zoomie leave Dr. M's last night," Tusk said. "I don't know if it was a girl or a boy—they were dressed as a squirrel or something."

Bobby slowly nodded. "Maaaaybe?" Then: "It's all a blank."

Tusk sighed. "We'll figure it out."

"Oh thank God," Bobby said. His admiration for Tusk's brain was boundless.

"Matt, go tell the others," Tusk said, thinking out loud now. "Devin and Tim should still be in their rooms. No, wait—Mrs. M is with Devin. I'm not sure we should say anything yet."

"Why is Mrs. M in Devin's room?" Bobby asked.

"Dude," Matt said. "It's Devin."

"Ohhhh."

"I don't want to be the one to tell her," Matt said to Tusk. "Maybe we could send a card. 'Condolences on the Murder of Your Scumbag Husband.'"

Tusk's ears fanned in annoyance. "Matt, *please*. Skip Devin's for now. Let Tim know what's happened, and tell him to stay in his room."

"That won't be hard."

"Kat may still be in there with him. She was babysitting him last night."

"Got it," Matt said. To Bobby he said, "Don't try to tongue-bath that shit. Take a shower."

"I don't lick myself!"

"Uh-huh." Matt loped out of the room.

"Look at me, Bobby," Tusk said. "The hotel's going to call the police, if they haven't already. One of the staff's already seen you, next to the body, covered in blood, which means they're going to question you first."

Bobby moaned.

"Don't panic," Tusk said. "Don't say anything until we get you some representation. When you do get to talk, you're going to tell the truth. You're just not going to tell *all* the truth."

"Like what?"

Tusk put his hands on Bobby's shoulders. "You know the things we don't talk about, right? Never ever talk about?"

Bobby nodded.

"That's still in effect. Now more than ever. But don't worry, I know you didn't kill Dr. M. We're going to get through this. As long as you listen to what I say."

"But what about the fans? What will they think? Will they still like me?"

Tusk draped his trunk around the back of Bobby's neck and pulled him close. It wasn't much of a trunk, less than a foot long, but it had its uses, and a comforting snuffle was one of them. "This is serious, Bobby. If we're not careful, you could end up going to jail."

"Oh man," Bobby said. "I'm going to need a really good publicist."

Track 2

"Catastrophe"

Featuring Detective Delgado

Detective Lucia Delgado wasn't happy to hear her phone ring. She'd finished her shift at 6:30 AM and was still in bed, still exhausted. She reached blindly for her Nokia, pulled it to her ear. Loud music played from the next room.

"Delgado," the voice said. "You should really answer your beeper."

Her beeper lay on the floor muffled in clothes. "This is my family number, Banks."

"I figured this was important enough."

"What is it?"

"Matador Grand. A bloody one."

It was her partner, Detective Mickey Banks. There'd been a homicide in the penthouse suite, and their captain wanted Delgado and Banks to lead the investigation team. She put two and two together (because that was her job) and said, "Let me guess. It's somebody famous."

Several years ago a teenage girl had overdosed in the car of a Beloved Film Icon, who then decided it would be really clever to make it appear as if the girl were alive several hours after he'd buried her in the desert. Luce not only solved the case but also got the actor to confess. Did they praise her for her ingenuity and tenaciousness? No. What really impressed her captain, the sheriff, and the mayor was that she knew how to talk to famous people and was good on television—neither of which should have been a surprise to anyone who knew how she grew up. Ever since that case she'd been designated the department's Celebrity Whisperer.

"Who is it?" she asked.

Banks said, "You're never going to believe it."

Luce called her sister and asked for an emergency babysit—the third such emergency in a month. "You don't even have to ask," Maria said. Which was a lie, but sweet.

Then Luce walked down the hall, past the rows of framed show posters, into her daughter's room—and into a wall of music. The boombox was blasting and Melanie was dancing furiously, singing along at the top of her voice.

When Luce was pregnant she told her husband that she didn't want to be like her parents. Melanie would get to choose her own likes and dislikes, follow her own passions, and she wouldn't be forced into the family business. Luce wasn't prepared for Melanie's first passion to be bubblegum pop. (She also wasn't prepared for her husband to leave her a year after Melanie was born, but fuck that lying piece of shit.)

It's a little too narratively convenient that her daughter was singing along with the WyldBoyZ at that moment, but it's the truth. She was soulfully belting out, "Deep down, I'm not hurtin'! Deep down, I'm not afraid!"

At least she was on key, Luce thought. Melanie had always had amazing pitch.

She was nine years old—dead center in the band's demographic sweet spot of preteen females—and a huge fan. A poster of the band—the one where they're wearing space suits from the *Unleashed* album—hung over her bed. Luce knew the names of every member of the band, because Melanie talked about them as if they were her personal friends. Devin, "the romantic one," was three-quarters bonobo; Tim, "the shy one," was a large percentage of pangolin; Matt, "the funny one," was a giant bat; and Tusk, "the smart one," was a hybrid elephant. Last but by no means least in the heart of Luce's daughter (and on the LVMPD person-of-interest list) was "the cute one," Bobby O.

Next to her mirror Melanie had pinned up a *Tiger Beat* cover filled with Bobby O's face. The headline read: "O Is for Ocelot! We Luv a Lot!" And indeed, Melanie *adored* him. Last week Luce was feeling bad she hadn't ponied up the $38.50 a ticket for the WyldBoyZ show at the Matador. She had zero interest in watching a bunch of genetically engineered manimals sing and dance like some Chuck E. Cheese nightmare, but Melanie would have lost her mind with joy. Now Luce was grateful she'd skipped.

"Sweetie. Stop it. Sweetie!"

Melanie kept twirling and kicking, not making eye contact, as if she knew what was coming. She was wearing a bright pink top, a floofy skirt over blue jeans, and UGGS knock-offs. Though she wasn't allowed to wear lipstick, she'd applied so much ChapStick that her lips glowed.

"Mommy's got to go to work," Luce said. "I need to drop you at Aunt Maria's, okay?"

She stopped dancing. "What?"

Luce turned off the boombox. "Pack your backpack. We'll go through the McDonald's drive-thru on the way there."

Melanie watched her mother's face, gauging how much she could get from her. But Luce was already wearing her Cop Face, so the odds weren't in Melanie's favor.

"I want a shake," Melanie said.

"Not for breakfast."

"It's *noon*!"

"Oh. Okay. Fine." In fact, it was 12:15. The body had been discovered by hotel staff forty-five minutes ago. Luce would have to ask her sister to keep Melanie away from the television—the case was going to be all over the news, and her favorite WyldBoy was the prime suspect.

Banks met Luce in front of the hotel. He was a lanky white kid with an enormous head—not yet thirty but already losing the battle with male pattern baldness. He'd joined Homicide and Sex Crimes only six months ago. A little too much of a smartypants, but he was eager, and trainable as a border collie. Part of his training was to have coffee waiting for her when she came on shift.

Luce took the paper cup from his hands and pushed through the glass doors into frigid air. The lobby was crowded with people in animal costumes.

Banks said, "It's a zoo in here."

She stared at him. "No comedy before coffee. What about the security footage?"

"I told the hotel manager not to let anyone touch it. He's a big fan of yours, by the way."

"Jesus Christ. Okay, let's get a CSD tech in there to lock it down."

They took the elevator to the penthouse. A pair of patrol officers guarded the hallway, which was covered by plastic sheeting. Three more loitered in front of the door to the victim's suite. She knew the cops' faces, if not their names, and they knew her by reputation.

"Where's our guy?" she asked one of them, meaning Bobby O. The ocelot-boy was in his room, being guarded (but not detained, in case any lawyer asked) by two officers. The other band members, as well as a female roadie and the victim's wife, had been told to stay in their rooms.

"Jesus, the wife's here, too?" Luce asked.

"Convenient," Banks said.

"We won't have any of them for long," she said. "Lawyers are on the march." Worse, the press would soon be here, and every paparazzi headhunter in Clark County. She told the patrolman to put out the order: no civilians in the stairwells or the elevator for the top two floors.

Inside the suite, half a dozen Crime Scene Detail people were picking their blue-gloved way over exposed surfaces like farmers of the microscopic. Luce wasn't sure what they could expect to find: There'd obviously been dozens of people partying in the suite last night and the place was awash in all manner of biological material. She stepped around a tech crouched over a piece of stereo equipment that had been torn from the wall, then followed the flashing lights to the master bedroom.

Inside was Lionel Paget, head of the CSD unit, instantly recognizable by the impressive wingspan of his gray handlebar moustache. Luce never understood how Lionel's facial hair was not a contaminant in every case in Las Vegas. Beside him, a photo tech was clicking away, capturing the corpse at all angles. It was a pretty big corpse, even with some of it gouged out.

"So." Banks. "*Somebody* was angry."

"I'd say you're right about that," Lionel said. He spoke in a cowboy drawl. If it was fake, he'd been faking it for the entire twenty years Luce had known him.

The furrows in Maurice Bendix's torso were deep. The T-shirt he'd been wearing was torn to shreds. The blood had soaked into the bed and through his sweatpants.

"Did you find the weapon?" Luce asked.

"No, ma'am," Lionel said.

"The cat guy does have claws," Banks said.

"So does half the band."

Luce asked for gloves, and then leaned close to the body and studied Dr. M's face. She pulled down one eyelid, then the other. Turned on her key-ring flashlight and peered into his nostrils. Then she peeled back an inch of his shirt to view one of the wounds. It was still seeping blood.

She straightened, looked at the bedside table. There was a small plastic tray, the kind restaurants use to hold receipts. She touched a gloved finger to it. There was some kind of white residue. "Get a few shots of this tray," she said to the woman with the camera. "Then have it bagged and tested."

The rest of the place looked like it had been ransacked—clothing all over the floor, drawers open—but she couldn't rule out that Bendix and his wife were slobs. The sliding glass door to the balcony was half-open, and a breeze stirred the air.

"You think robbery, too?" Luce asked Lionel.

"Cat burglar," Banks said.

"I don't reckon," Lionel said. "We found jewelry and a wallet full of cash in the bathroom. But there was blood on some of the clothing on the floor and in the luggage, like they was rummaging around."

Luce reached into Lionel's supply duffel, grabbed a few evidence bags for herself, as well as a packet of swabs and extra gloves, and jammed it all into her pockets. Then she walked back into the lounge and headed toward the balcony and those billowing white drapes. Dark spots flecked the material. "Did anybody see the stains on this?" she asked. One of the techs said he'd get on it.

Luce stepped onto the balcony and Banks followed. The sun was bright and the wind was strong. A couple of ring-billed seagulls hung in the air just six feet from the balcony, riding the updraft. She wondered if the hotel guests fed them. In Las Vegas, even the birds made their living from the tourists. The next balcony, the one connected to the master bedroom, was a dozen feet away.

Banks leaned over the edge. "Long way down. That's the way I would have done it. Tossed him over the side."

"Did you see the size of him?" she asked.

"The elephant man could handle it, I bet. And the gorilla."

"Bonobo."

"Oh my goodness," Banks said. "You're a fan."

"Melanie loves them." About then she noticed the sliding door. A web of cracks radiated from an impact point. "Something hit the door pretty hard."

"That would explain the blood on the curtains. Do you think it's part of this? There was a party here—somebody could have hit it then."

"Right." This place was going to be a mess, physical-evidence wise. "Let's go talk to Bobby O."

She grabbed a couple patrolmen standing inside the room, told them to go down to the lobby and start asking for people who'd been at the party. "Get names and IDs before they all fly back to fucking Indiana."

Before either one of them could move, a woman started screaming.

By this point in Luce's career she was a connoisseur of screams, especially of the Las Vegas variety: the ecstatic Holy-Shit I-Rolled-a-Hard-Eight!; the shocked There's-a-Drunk-Guy-Peeing-in-the-Elevator; the pain-filled and panicked Oh-My-God-a-Lexus-Backed-over-My-Foot (only heard once, but memorable). This scream was one she recognized instantly: Entitled-White-Lady-Demanding-Badge-Numbers.

The screamer was a fiftyish redhead, body by Pilates, hair and boobs courtesy of other expensive technologies. Her miniskirt was shrink-wrapped to her, and her spangled spaghetti-string top was as understated as one of Luce's daughter's outfits.

"It's my goddamn room!" the woman shouted. She saw the cops glance at Luce and immediately shifted her attack. "You! Tell these *goons* to get out of my way, or so help me—"

"You're Mrs. Bendix?" Luce asked.

"Of course I am."

"Ma'am, I'm sorry to tell you this, but your husband—"

"For Christ sake, I know he's dead. I want to see the body!"

"I'm sorry, ma'am," Luce said. "I can't let you do that."

That pissed off the widow even more. Her smeared mascara added to the sense of demented outrage. "I'm his *wife*. So legally, that's *my room*."

Behind her, various heads peeked out of doorways. Five sets of eyes and a grab bag of other features: a gray trunk, a black snout, dark fur, steel-colored scales.... There was one 100 percent human face, belonging to the female roadie Luce had been told about, though even hers was nonstandard: Dark geometric tattoos marked her from the forehead down. The corridor looked like an old-timey illustration of the Barnum & Bailey zoo train, plus hipster conductor.

"All of you!" Luce barked. "Please stay in your rooms. We're going to come talk to you as soon as we can, but right now, you've got to let us do our work."

The widow started to open her mouth and Luce silenced her with a raised hand. "What room were you in last night?"

She blinked. "Last night?"

Down the hall, the ape face suddenly ducked out of sight.

Luce gestured to one of the patrolmen. "This officer will walk you back there." As he passed she gave him a look that couldn't be mistaken: *And make sure she fucking stays there.*

Track 3

"Party Animal"

Featuring Bobby O

The blood had stiffened Bobby's fur into bristles and the urge to lick himself clean was almost unbearable. The uniformed cops had allowed him to put on a hotel bathrobe, planted him on the couch, and told him not to move. He wondered if this included nontraditional self-care. Their uniforms and their aggression reminded Bobby of the security guards back on the barge, who'd not been shy about keeping order with electric cattle prods. Bobby often woke from nightmares with the smell of burning fur in his nose.

A dark-haired woman walked in, followed by a tall guy who seemed to be 40 percent forehead. Both of them carried coffee cups, but they hadn't brought any for him. Not that he liked coffee, but it would have been polite. They looked around at the room. Bobby had wrecked the place pretty good last night. The coffee table was turned over, the giant TV screen was all starry, and the couch pillows were torn to shreds.

"Are you my lawyers?" Bobby asked hopefully.

"No, I'm Detective Delgado and this is Detective Banks," the woman said. "We'd like to ask you a few questions."

"Am I under arrest?" He started to breathe hard.

"No, not at all," Delgado said. "You're free to leave at any time." She glanced at the claw marks in the white leather seat opposite him and sat down anyway. "I'd like to make sure you're all right, though. Are you cut at all? Hurt?"

"I don't think so."

"Better safe than sorry." She asked the uniformed cops to give them the room and told them to radio for paramedics. To Bobby she said, "Just as a precaution."

"But—"

"You know, my daughter's a huge fan of yours."

"Really?"

"She says you're the best dancer."

"Well, *yaaah!*" Bobby grinned, then remembered his media training. "But we all work as a team. Choreo is like singing harmony—if one person's a little off, it just doesn't work, you know? Some of the parts are greater than the . . . whole part."

"Truer words," Detective Banks said.

"We'd like to help you out, Bobby," Delgado said. "But I have to tell you, it looks pretty bad. It seems like last night's party got a little out of control."

"It *was* pretty great," Bobby said. "I mean, except for the murder part."

"Why don't you tell us about it. When did you get there?"

"I was there at the start?" Then he had to explain that the actual start was backstage, with lots of people stopping by, lots of drinking, and had continued on the bus to the hotel (a short ride, but thanks to the bus's stripper pole and a zoomie wearing a cat fursuit—kind of a tribute to Bobby, really—an awesome fifteen minutes), and then it was up to the penthouse floor.

The detectives had notebooks out, and they kept asking for names and times—who was on the bus, did they arrive at the hotel by midnight or 12:30, who came up to the room—but Bobby had never been good at keeping track of people and/or time. "I'm kind of an in-the-now person," he explained.

"Sure," Banks said. "You're an artist."

"Right!"

"Was Dr. M on the bus?" Delgado asked.

"No, he had his own car—he hates the bus. The whole time we were on tour, he never rode on it."

"How long have you been on tour?"

"Um, seven years?"

"What?"

"I mean, mostly? Except when we were recording and rehearsing—it's been pretty much nonstop since Dr. M took us on. He says that if you're not the top, you're the bottom, and he will not be fucked by Joey Fatone."

"Who's Joey Fatone?" Banks asked.

"NSYNC? Justin Timberlake?" The detectives looked at him blankly. Did they not know anything? "It doesn't matter, all those guys want to fuck us. NSYNC, the Backstreet Boys, Boyz II Men, Menudo, Westlife—"

"*Menudo's* still around?" Banks asked.

"Those guys are unstoppable! They restock every year. As soon as one of them hits puberty—*whick!*—they pop in a new guy. Dr. M says they raise them on a farm."

"A Menudo farm," Delgado said.

"I think it's in Mexico. No offense."

Delgado stared at him. "Let's get back to the party."

"I remember everything!" Bobby said.

The party really took off once the band got to the penthouse. Jay-Z was thundering on the massive sound system, zoomies were dancing and rubbing on each other, and everybody wanted to share their drugs. Dr. M sat in this huge spinning leather chair, giving rides to half-naked hot girls and hotter boys. Their abs were so defined they looked like they'd been drawn in Sharpie.

"So who's next?" Dr. M called out. His wide face was flushed from spinning. "I need a dancer. Who's a dancer? Wait, *all* of you?"

At one point Tusk stomped over and told Bobby to chill out. Bobby was ten feet in the air, perched on top of a rack of lights, which was suspended above the pool table by two thin cables. The rack was swaying, but Bobby kept his balance, aided by two bottles of vodka, one in each hand. People around the table were chanting, "Max-ee-mum! Max-ee-mum!"

"Bobby. Come down. You're going to hurt yourself."

Bobby hissed at him, and everybody laughed. "I am the highest!" Bobby said. "I am *literally* the highest."

"Who taught him a new word?" Tusk asked. One of the fans sheepishly raised a hand.

"Kat, can you help?" Tusk asked. "Kat!"

But Kat couldn't hear him over the music. She was standing by the wall with Tim, holding his claw. Tim, per usual at any event with more than two people, looked stressed out. One of his great fears was that a fan would pluck one of his precious scales. It was such a stupid phobia, because it had only happened twice. Okay, maybe three times, but only in China!

Only Kat could soothe him when he was like this. She looked as intimidatingly cool as always: She was wearing her standard uniform of mechanic's coveralls and combat boots, and her facial tattoos gave her a default expression of Back the Fuck Off, which was handy for keeping the zoomies from crowding Tim. Kat did all the hard jobs, and managing Tim was one of the hardest. He puked before every performance, shook when he talked to the media, and avoided parties, especially ones where fans might get in. Why did he come to this one if he was just going to mope? He looked like he wanted to curl into a ball—literally.

Tusk lifted his arms. "Come on, buddy."

Bobby said, "Promise me this isn't the last time."

"It's not the last time."

"We're always going to hang out together, right?"

"The band's breaking up," Tusk said. "Not *us*."

"The fuck it is." Dr. M had risen from his chair. He was bedecked in band paraphernalia: WBZ sweat pants, WyldBoyZ Unleashed 2000 Tour tank-top T, Signature Tusk elephant-feet slippers, and the WBZ healing crystal amulet that Devin insisted be sold at every concert. It all looked terrible on the Doc, and it broke the unwritten Rule of Cool that band members should never wear their own merch. It was so uncool, Bobby thought, that it crossed the line back into cool. Dr. M didn't give a fuck!

Dr. M looked up at Tusk and said, "Nobody's breaking up until I say so."

Somebody cut the music right before that moment, and so the entire room heard him.

Tusk said, "We can talk about this in the morning."

"What, with your lawyers? Are you going to go through with this fucking lawsuit?"

"Maury, please."

"You think you can do anything without me? You can't even get Bobby down from the fucking ceiling!" He dug into the pockets of his sweat pants. "You want to get him down? Here." His hand came up with a CD. "No, not that. This." From his other pocket he pulled out a large Baggie of white powder. "Here, kitty kitty! Daddy's got a treat!"

"Finally!" Bobby said. He dropped onto the pool table. Dropped one of the bottles of vodka onto the table and reached for the Baggie.

Dr. M backed up, jiggling. "All the way down, Bobby, there ya go."

Bobby hopped to the floor and snatched the Baggie from his hand. "Woo-hoo!"

Then, suddenly, the Baggie vanished. Kat had grabbed it from him. "Hey!" Bobby shouted.

Kat was a small woman, barely over five feet tall, but no one crossed her, especially not the boyz. She shoved the Baggie at Dr. M. "Keep that shit to yourself."

Bobby loved that Kat's accent got especially strong when she was angry.

"Watch yourself, bitch," Dr. M said.

"What did you say to me?" Kat said.

"I trusted you! You fucking two-faced—"

Tim yelled, "Take that back!"

Dr. M started bellowing at Tim; Kat shouted back. Tusk pleaded for calmness. Bobby edged toward Dr. M, eyeing the Baggie in his hand.

Then: a shriek. It only lasted for a second or two, but everyone covered their ears.

The crowd turned. Matt's wings were spread under his poncho. "Party's over!" Matt announced. "Thanks for attending, please pick up your gift bags on the way out."

"Fuck you, Matt!" Dr. M shouted. "This party's not over till I say so." He strode toward the wall with the sound system. Fursuited zoomies scattered out of his way. He punched a button, and a five-disc CD tray slid out. He dropped in the CD he'd been holding.

"Listen to this, motherfuckers."

The speakers popped and the room filled with the synthesizer cords and a nasal voice: "Saaaaailing takes me away to where I've always—"

"Fuck, wrong CD." Dr. M punched the button and the song cut off.

"Aw, I was almost asleep," Matt said.

The speakers came alive again: a solo voice, singing wordlessly. The voice was high-pitched, pure. Then, another voice joined in, and another, and another. At first it was a moving, three-note chord, but suddenly it split into six notes, and the harmony shifted.

"That's enough," Tusk said.

"I own this," Dr. M said. "And I own all of you."

Kat reached toward the sound system and Dr. M grabbed her arm. "Back off, Kat. I own you, too."

Tim screamed something and threw himself into Dr. M. The big man fell backwards, shouting, "Get him off me!" and then everyone was shouting. One of the fans—a zebra whose name was Sweater or Swetta or something—wailed in alarm. Nobody liked to see their parents fight.

The music cut off mid-note. Kat pulled Tim off the Doc, and Matt stepped between the Doc and Kat, keeping them apart with his impressive wingspan.

Kat said something into Tim's ear, then turned him and pointed him toward the door. Bobby heard her say, "You want to build your fort now, buddy? Let's go build you a fort."

Matt helped Dr. M to his feet. He was gasping and clutching his chest.

A female voice said, "What the fuck are you doing, Maury?"

It was Mrs. M. She was wrapped in a towel, and her very wet red hair was piled atop her head. Beside her stood Devin, just as wet, but with decidedly no towel. His fur was sleek and his penis seemed happy to be invited to the party.

"People, people," Devin said. "Why is everyone so angry?"

"Get the fuck out of my room," Dr. M said. He pointed at Devin. "And get your stinking paws off her, you damn dirty—"

"Dude!" Devin said. "*Dude.*"

Dr. M stumbled toward the back bedroom. Bobby thought, Cocaine? Hello, cocaine?

Tusk put a hand on him. "Come on, Bobby. We're going."

"What? We can't leave now, the party's just getting interesting!" He lifted his hands and realized there was still a bottle of Smirnoff in one of them. He took a swig. "Yow! We have not yet begun to rock!"

Tusk drew him into a hug.

"Aw, I love you, too," Bobby said.

Tusk tightened his arms and carried Bobby toward the door.

Track 4

"Lock Up My Heart
(and Throw Away the Key)"

Featuring Detective Delgado

"After that," said the genetically engineered ocelot-human hybrid, "it all gets a bit fuzzy."

Bobby O blinked his big eyes. His whiskers twitched hopefully. The small hairs of his pointy ears caught the light from the window.

Jesus Christ, Luce thought, even painted with blood, he was adorable. No wonder her daughter loved him best.

Luce looked at Banks to see how he was doing with all this. It was his first high-profile homicide and she was worried he'd be distracted, but his pencil was moving at speed.

Banks said, "What time do you think it was when Tusk carried you out of the party?"

"No idea," Bobby said. "Two? Three?"

Luce asked, "Did Tusk take you directly back to your room?"

"Yeah. And then I kept trying to come out, but he was blocking the door. For, like, forever."

"He stayed outside your door?" Banks asked.

"He wouldn't leave! He said something about me having had enough, which, like, fair. But then I remembered the mini-bar. Do you know they stock that thing every night? Anyway, after the tiny bottles were gone, I was pretty out of it, but I kept thinking about Dr. M."

"You mean, Dr. M's drugs," Luce said.

"Yeah, that."

"So how did you get back into his room?"

Bobby let them in on his current theory.

"You . . . jumped," Luce said. "From balcony to balcony." She glanced at Banks. His mouth was hanging open.

"I'm a pretty good jumper," Bobby said.

"While you were *drunk*."

"I wouldn't try that shit while I was straight! Did you know we're fifty-seven stories up?"

Luce took a breath. "So. You somehow got onto one of the balconies. Do you remember which one?"

"Which what?"

"There are two balconies," Luce said in a patient voice. "One for the master bedroom, one for the living room. Do you remember which room you stepped into?"

"Ummm, no. That's a blank."

"Do you remember hitting anything?" Luce said. "Running into, say, a wall or door?"

"I just remember being in Dr. M's room and looking down at this tray of powder. That's, like, really clear. Have you ever wanted something really badly, and then you just *get* it? Like, you're really hungry for pizza, and then a guy comes to your door and you open the box and it's full of cocaine? It was like that."

"Then you snorted a bunch of this cocaine—"

"*Oh* yeah."

"—and just . . . passed out?"

Bobby searched his memory. "Seems like." He caught Luce and Banks glancing at each other. "What?"

"That's not the usual side effect," Banks said.

"Huh," Bobby said. He shrugged. "It was a long night."

Luce let Banks ask the next questions. Did Bobby have a beef with Dr. M? Did maybe they fight when Bobby broke into the hotel room? Had he ever lost control and clawed somebody?

"No, no, and once," Bobby answered. "Okay, maybe twice, but it was an accident both times. But I didn't touch Dr. M! Did Tusk tell you about the zoomie?"

"The what now?" Luce asked.

"The zoomie! The fan? There was a girl in Dr. M's room, after the party. Or maybe a boy. They were in costume."

"Did *you* see this person?" Luce said.

"I want to say yes."

"But . . ."

Bobby sighed. "I can't remember."

The door opened and one of the uniformed cops came in, followed by a man in a suit. Luce blew out her lips. It was Caleb Mills of Mills, Milsap, and Newton, the local one-stop shop for high rollers who found themselves in deep shit.

"Afternoon, Detective," Mills said. "Could you stop talking to my client now?"

"Are *you* my lawyer?" Bobby asked.

"I am indeed. Did you ask for a lawyer and they kept talking to you?"

"He asked *if* we were his lawyers," Luce said.

"That's true," Bobby said.

Mills sighed. "Okay, let's go, Bobby."

"Not so fast." Luce stood up. "Bobby O, you are under arrest for the murder of Dr.—is he really a doctor?"

"Kinda like Dr. Dre is a doctor?" Bobby said.

"Maurice Bendix," Luce finished. "Banks, cuff him and read him his rights."

Bobby felt woozy. All the words Detective Banks said were familiar. The boyz had watched a lot of American TV on the barge.

"Don't say anything without me there, okay, Bobby?" the lawyer said.

"Okay." Bobby looked at Luce. "Do you want me to sign something?"

"For God's sake, no!" the lawyer said.

"Usually I just do a picture or a T-shirt," Bobby said to her.

Luce was confused.

"Just tell me your daughter's name," Bobby said patiently.

"Oh," she said. "I'm sure there'll be plenty of time for autographs later."

———

Delgado and Banks escorted Bobby out of the room. Tusk filled the doorway across the hall. His gigantic gray head, made larger by those fanlike ears, sat atop an imposing body. He would have been terrifying if it weren't for the fact that he was wearing a well-tailored suit.

"Don't worry, Bobby," Tusk said. "You didn't do anything. You'll be okay."

Another door opened. A narrow black face topped in a golden fuzz—Matt M. Bat. "Hang in there," he said.

Luce heard a pounding behind her. A figure charged forward on all fours, screeching. One of the uniformed cops shouted, "Stop!" It was Devin, black fur wet and gleaming. He was naked from the waist up. Luce stepped in front of him before he reached Bobby.

The ape abruptly stopped his charge, just inches from her. He looked up at her, shook his long, David Cassidy hair, and regarded her with those famously soulful brown eyes. He'd evidently just stepped out of the shower, and he smelled *amazing*—a mix of citrus, cedar, and ex-boyfriend who just worked out.

"I want to say good-bye," he said.

"Say good-bye from there," Luce answered.

The bonobo leaned around her. "Bobby. Think calming thoughts. My spirit is with yours."

"Thanks, man!"

Luce managed to get Bobby to the elevator without further incident. She told the two cops who'd been guarding him in his room to take him downtown for booking, but not to let anyone talk to him.

Luce turned to address the hallway: "Everyone, please stay in your rooms. We'll come talk to you individually." She looked at Devin. "Please be fully dressed."

Track 5

"Heavy Petting"

Featuring Devin

Devin *intended* to go back to his room—until Mrs. M pushed past him, marched into Tusk's suite, and started shouting. Devin glanced at Matt. He was draped in one of his ridiculous Argentinian ponchos. He looked like Clint Eastwood, if Clint Eastwood were a giant bat. Matt said, "We can't miss this."

Tusk had settled into the huge leather chair Kat had ordered up special for him, and let Mrs. M's anger wash over him. She accused Tusk of murdering Dr. M, of trying to steal his money and hers, and of various other crimes. Devin tried to soothe her, but then she turned her rage on him. This was unfair; just this morning he'd given her a beautiful orgasm.

Devin slumped onto the couch and tried to label the emotions churning within him, as his therapist and acting teacher had taught him to do (in L.A. he'd found a terrific woman who was both a licensed psychologist and SAG member). His mind kept circling back to Tusk's special chair, and the size of this multi-room suite. Yes, Tusk was as big as a Volvo, but why did he always score the biggest room outside of Dr. M's? Did Kat love him more?

Devin took a cleansing breath. Jealousy was the soul-killer. He needed to get in touch with his purer, nobler self and then give the gift of his own serenity to the room.

A voice said, "God damn it! What did I say?"

Devin opened his eyes. The detectives had returned. The female one—Delgado, an intriguing name, he was pretty sure it meant "the cat"—was surveying the room, and when she looked at him he felt a charge pass between them. She frowned, and he thought, That's right. Cover it up. Be a professional.

"Fine, since you're all here," she said. "Wait, where's Tim?"

"Probably hiding," Devin said.

"He's having a little bit of a breakdown," Matt explained. He was looming behind the couch in his Matt way.

"Do I need to send someone?" Delgado asked.

"It's kind of a daily thing," Matt said.

"Kat's with him," Tusk said.

Banks looked up from his notepad. "Kat's the roadie?"

"Road *Manager*," Matt said. "The Queen of the Roadies."

"All right, fine," Delgado said. "I'll talk to them separately."

Devin stood up, and Detective Banks put a hand on his holster. Devin held up his hands. "Dude. Please." Devin understood that he could look intimidating—people had read way too many stories about chimps ripping people's arms off—which was why he took pains to exude calm.

"I'd like to say a few words," Devin said.

"Please sit down," Banks said.

"This is a dark day," Devin said. "Tragedy has struck our little family. I think we should have a moment of silence to honor a departed soul, a man who—"

Matt snorted. "Soul."

"Everybody has a soul, Matt!" Devin said. "Why do you have to ruin everything?"

"Sit *down*," Delgado said. "Please. This is not the time."

Devin took a breath. "I was just trying to help." He sat on the couch—beside Mrs. M. She didn't look at him.

"Where did you take Maury's body?" she asked Delgado. "I saw you wheel him out of here."

"I hope the fans didn't see him," Devin said.

"If I see pictures in the press, I'll sue," Mrs. M said.

"The body was fully covered," Delgado answered. "If you want one of our people to drive you over to the hospital, we can do that. I know this has been a shock, for all of you. We all want to find out what happened to Maurice, and with your cooperation we can do that, I hope quickly."

"You already arrested Bobby," Mrs. M said.

"Bobby didn't do it," Devin said. "He's a gentle soul under all that . . . excitability. He could never do that to Dr. M."

"I second that," Tusk said.

"He's an annoying little bastard," Matt said. "But he wouldn't murder someone."

"Not even coked up to his gills?" Banks asked.

"Who told you about his gills?" Matt asked.

"Does he really—?"

"He's a catfish," Matt said.

"To be clear," Tusk said, addressing the detectives. "Bobby does not have gills."

"Ooh, Tusk, tell them about the zoomie!" Devin said. "Tusk saw a fan leave Dr. M's room last night after the—yow!" The tip of a wing had flicked Devin's ear. Matt rolled his eyes toward Mrs. M. Oh, right, Devin thought. Widow.

"Fan?" Banks asked.

"Who was Maury fucking last night?" Mrs. M demanded.

"I'd prefer to talk to the detectives about that in private," Tusk said. "But it does bring up the point that there must be other suspects, besides us."

"What?" Devin exclaimed. "Us?" Nothing in this meeting was going like he expected.

"Everyone! *Please*," Delgado said. Everyone immediately shut up, and Devin felt a thrill run through him. Nothing was more attractive than charisma.

"Please stop talking among yourselves," Delgado said. "We'll be interviewing all of you individually. Yes, we did arrest Bobby, but we still need to get a full understanding of what happened, and when, and of course we are open to all possibilities. None of you are suspects, but you are all, as of now, material witnesses. You're not allowed to leave the city, and I'd prefer you to stay in this hotel."

"You can't keep us here," Mrs. M said. "That's illegal!"

"No," Tusk said. "It's not."

"Mr. . . . Tusk is right," Banks said. "We can arrest you if you don't comply."

"But I'm sure it won't come to that," Delgado said. "All we're asking for right now is that you stay in your rooms until we can take your statements."

"I want my things," Mrs. M said. "My luggage is in the suite."

"I'll have our people get that to you."

"I also want that police escort to the hospital—and after I get back, I want my own room. On another floor."

"Why?" Devin said. Then quickly added, "Of course! Everyone should have their own room. Why *would* we share rooms?"

Tusk rubbed a hand over his big gray forehead. Devin knew

that look: *Hit your notes, Devin. Hit your marks, Devin. Don't hit on the fans, Devin.* But just because Tusk was the oldest of the boyz, that didn't make him the boss.

Devin had his own dreams, and they had nothing to do with five-part harmony and synchronized dance moves and shared residuals. Was it his fault that he was more human looking than the rest of them and had more career options? No! Would he allow guilt and brotherly devotion to divert him from his journey of self-actualization? Hell no!

Dr. M had kept them all in a cage. "Unleashed" was a joke. They were all chained by their egregious contracts.

It was time to throw off those chains and go solo. All Devin had to do to make it happen was avoid being accused of Dr. M's murder.

———————

Devin's room was emptier without Mrs. M. Also, the tub of trail mix specified in his rider was dangerously low. He scooped out a handful of nuts and cranberries and hoped Mrs. M's feelings for him hadn't changed just because her husband had been brutally murdered.

When the knock came, Devin did not immediately answer. He dusted off his hands, took a cleansing breath, and reached for a sense memory of a sad moment in his past. Something from the tour? Nothing occurred to him. Earlier, maybe? Perhaps on the barge—

screaming fire water blood cold

Shit! No! Too far!

They knocked again. Devin exhaled. Opened the door.

Detective Delgado, with Detective Banks behind her. Delgado's eyes narrowed. "Are you okay?"

"I'm fine," Devin said. "Grief. It sneaks up on you, you know?" There were tears in his eyes. Tears! Good job, Devin. He hopped onto the bed and looped his arms around his knees. He'd taken care to dress in a classy but not classist manner: a Tom Ford tuxedo-style shirt open to his navel, low-rise Roberto Cavalli jeans, and a pair of fabulous $1,500 hemp sandals woven by a certified-Native-American craftswoman.

Banks took one of the only two chairs in the ridiculously small room. Delgado had paused in front of a painting—she'd noticed his artwork!

"It's in my rider," Devin said. "I won't sleep in a room unless my own pieces are hanging. I painted all of them."

"This woman looks familiar," Delgado asked.

"That's Barbara Bush! You didn't recognize her?"

"I've never seen her nude."

Banks showed him a microcassette recorder. "You mind if I record this?"

"As long as you set the levels right," Devin said. "I'm more of a bass than people realize." He smiled winningly.

Banks flinched. Devin thought, Too much teeth!

"Why don't you tell us about last night?" Banks asked.

"I don't know what there is to tell you," Devin said. "I left the party before anything happened."

Banks said, "Give it a shot."

"Well, I spent most of the party in the Jacuzzi. I find that after a performance a good soak does wonders."

Devin heard the balcony door open behind him. Delgado had stepped out and was looking up, toward the roof.

"And Mrs. Bendix was in the Jacuzzi with you?" Banks asked.

"And others," he said. "But yes, that's right. We're friends."

"Or more than friends," Banks said.

"What do you mean?"

"She stayed the night here with you, yes?" Banks said.

"That's right. We left the party together."

"When did you leave?"

"Right after the big fight. Mrs. M wanted to leave, so we walked out."

"In your towels?"

"Right. It's no big deal, I mean, we're right down the hall."

"And you came straight here."

"We did. And we stayed here, all night, until Tusk came and told us the news."

"Mrs. Bendix will be able to confirm that?" he asked.

"Sure," Devin said. "I mean, we were asleep *some* of the time."

Banks all but rolled his eyes.

"Did she often stay with you?" Delgado asked. Devin liked that there was no judgement in her voice—unlike her partner. She'd been gazing at another of his nudes, the one he'd titled *Jane Goodall, Rampant.*

"It's happened a couple of times before, sure," Devin said.

Banks asked, "How long have you two been in a relationship?"

"I've been in *relationship* since I met her. All of us are in relationships. You and I are in a relationship now. What kind of relationship, well, we can explore that together."

"Answer the question," Banks said. Ooh, he was touchy. Maybe insecure in his own sexuality? Very interesting.

"Our relationship became physical about a week ago," Devin said. "I mean, she had hit on me plenty of times, and

Tusk always told me to stay away from her. But then, I realized, hey, she's a beautiful woman who deserves happiness. The tour was ending. We should just do this, you know? And wow, was I surprised. She's an older woman, but her upper body strength, her *stamina*, it's just . . ." He shook his head. "We did some positions I didn't know were possible. Do you know she used to be a pole dancer?"

"I'm shocked," Banks said. "Did Dr. M know about the affair?"

Affair. Such a value-laden word. "We weren't *hiding* it," Devin said.

"How did the doctor feel about that?"

Devin wished Banks would stop asking the questions. It was Delgado he'd like to talk to.

"I don't put a lot of energy into negative feelings like jealousy and possessiveness," Devin said. "But some people . . . do. I don't understand it. Especially because Dr. M fucked around. Why would he be jealous of Mrs. M?"

"Maybe it's because she's his wife," Banks said, "and you're, well—"

"What? An animal? Is this about Alabama?" Devin was standing now, his arms out. "They dropped the case! No charges."

"*Young*," Banks finished.

"Oh," Devin said. He lowered his arms. "That's true."

"What happened in Alabama?" Banks asked.

"Let's stay on track," Delgado said. She took the seat next to Banks. "Was Dr. M sleeping with anyone last night?"

"Probably. He usually picked out a zoomie. Or two."

"Think about last night," she said. "Was there anyone in particular he'd 'picked out'?"

"Sorry, I wasn't hanging with him. Like I said—Jacuzzi. But you should talk to Tusk. He saw someone."

"We will. What got you and Mrs. Bendix to leave the tub and join the main party?" she asked.

"Mostly the screaming," Devin said. "Matt did one of his shrieks, and then people were shouting at each other. Mrs. M wanted to see what was going on. By the time we got out there the energy in the room was very negative and the party was breaking up."

"Did you hear the CD that Dr. M played?" Delgado asked.

"Um, a bit."

"Did you recognize it?"

"It sounded like us, but it must have been an outtake or something. Not a quality track."

"What makes one 'quality'?"

"All our top-selling songs are centered around my vocals," Devin explained. "My job is to be the spine, the anchor, the emotional heart. The other guys support what I'm doing, vocally, and yes, they have their own solos, but for most of our songs they're essentially backup singers."

"Right," Delgado said. "So it wasn't you on that recording?"

"I only heard a snippet, and that was over the roar of the Jacuzzi. Maybe I'm in there? But honestly it sounds like something Tusk left on the cutting room floor—not true WyldBoyZ, you know?"

"Dr. M seemed to think it was," Banks said. He looked at his notepad. "He said he owned the music, and owned the band—he owned all of you."

Devin looked pained. "Dr. M, like many human males, is trapped in a hierarchical mindset—the fear of not being an alpha male."

"Human males," Banks repeated.

"So *does* he own all the music?" Delgado asked.

"He's on the albums as a co-writer, but that's just on paper. He didn't write anything, that's all Tusk and Tim. Tusk does the music, and Tim does the words."

"Tusk does all the music?" Delgado asked.

"Basically." Devin explained how Tusk came into the studio with a head full of music, everything worked out in his mind: melodies, harmonies, percussion, even string arrangements. He'd teach the melody to Devin and the harmonies to the others, and Tim would sit in a corner and write lyrics. The rest of the album would be recorded with studio musicians. Tusk supervised that, as well as the mixing and editing. "He's a huge gray pain in the ass," Devin said, "but I got to admit he's a musical genius."

"I didn't realize so much depended on him," Delgado said.

"Oh, well, of course we all contribute to the songs," Devin said. "For example, on 'Get Away' I improvised the popping noise on the pre-chorus. And in 'One of a Kind' I improvised the popping noise in the second verse. It sounds just like a pistol."

"And what did Dr. M contribute?" Delgado asked.

"Tension, mostly."

Delgado smiled indulgently, and Devin thought, She likes me! Your armor is cracking, Detective.

"He *was* tense!" Devin said. "I tried to keep things calm, because I'm really the peacemaker in the group. But Dr. M was always ramped up about how much time Tusk was spending in the studio, how much everything cost, how every moment we weren't on the road was lost income. But he couldn't help us with the songs. He didn't know how to play an instrument, couldn't sing, didn't write lyrics, he couldn't even run a sound-board. Yet he got a huge cut."

Delgado leaned forward, and the top of her blouse opened slightly. Her intensity was captivating.

"So, what's going to happen with—" She glanced down, then leaned back in her chair. "Jesus Christ."

"Happen with what?" Devin asked innocently.

"The lawsuit, Devin. What's going to happen with the lawsuit against Dr. M?"

"I don't know, Tusk handles all that."

"Don't play dumb," Banks said. "Hey. Look at me. Does Mrs. Bendix get her husband's share of the rights?"

"I suppose so. We haven't talked about it. We're going day by day, experience by experience, staying open to the possibilities. She said she'd help finance my passion project. Getting the rights is going to be tricky, but it'll blow people's minds." He leaned forward. "*Inherit the Wind*," he said. "*The Musical.*"

"Wow," said Banks.

Devin beamed. "I'll play the Clarence Darrow part."

"You plan on shaving?" Banks asked.

"I say this with love," Devin said. "I don't like you."

Delgado said, "Was one of the possibilities you and Mrs. M getting married?"

"What? Whoa."

"I'm just wondering if you've talked about it," she said.

He thought a moment. "I'm not going to rule that out, but . . . then again, she is in love with me."

"A marriage would give you two the majority of profits from the band," Banks said.

"I guess, but that's not what our relationship is about."

"So now that Dr. M is dead, will you still go through with the suit?" Delgado asked.

"I don't know," Devin said. "I guess that depends on Mrs. M." A thought occurred to him. "Are you . . . do you think that *I* had something to do with this?"

"One last question," Banks said. "How good are you at climbing? It seems like it would be your thing."

"That's racist," Devin said. "And I want my lawyer."

"Girl, You Take Me Higher"

Featuring Detective Delgado

Luce closed the door behind her. Banks started to speak and she said, "Over here." She led him toward the stairwell.

Banks said, "Did that asshole have a *boner*?"

"Don't worry, I was ready to spray him with the hose," Luce said.

"I was surprised you wanted to talk to him first," Banks said.

"Something about seeing him with Mrs. M, and what you said about him being a climber," she said. "You ever read the Edgar Allan Poe story 'The Murders in the Rue Morgue'?"

"What's it about?"

"The first locked-room mystery. It involves a baboon with a straight razor."

"Ooh! Are we in a locked-room mystery?"

"We were, for about ten seconds. Then the first suspect is a guy who can jump fifteen feet, and the next one's an ape. Now it's just . . . weird."

"Science fiction, then."

"Oh God, I hope not."

"Devin would have no trouble with the physical part,"

Banks said. "That guy is shredded."

"It doesn't work. Devin's room is on the other side of the hallway, and the wall is sheer glass. There's no way he can jump balcony to balcony like Bobby, though—shit."

"What? You've got that look on your face."

"Let's go see the roof."

They walked up another story and pushed through the crash bar. Banks held the door so it wouldn't close behind them.

The roof, like that of most commercial buildings in Las Vegas, was painted a brilliant white. The heat and light were intense, but at least there was a breeze. Two flags snapped in the wind: the Stars and Stripes and below it the all-but-all-blue Nevada state flag. Luce walked amongst the boxy air-conditioning units, peering closely at their sides. Everything seemed to be freshly painted.

"You want to tell me what you're looking for?" Banks called.

"Don't worry," she said. "I'm not going to find it."

She walked to the edge of the roof, looked down at the wall of glass she'd been looking up at from Devin's balcony. It was a thirty- or forty-foot drop to the balcony. She walked to the other side and looked down at the balconies on that side: two for the penthouse, a wide one attached to the lounge, and the smaller one outside the master bedroom. To the right of that was the balcony to Bobby's room, and then Matt's.

She looked back across the roof at the flagpole. It was ringed by box lights, which were off at the moment. She stepped over the ring of lights and peered at the base of the pole. Flecks of white paint lay on the black base. Two or so feet above the base, the white paint on the pole had been scraped off. The scraping traveled most of the way around the pole.

Luce walked back to Banks and they started down. She told him what she'd seen.

"Which means what?" he asked.

"Someone attached a rope. Mountain-climbing gear, maybe. I could picture a metal carabiner scraping the paint."

"Devin *climbed*? I knew it."

"It's possible. Sometime before the party or at the start of it, he could go up to the roof the way we did and drop the rope down to his balcony. After the party, he could climb up, cross the roof, then go down to Dr. M's. The timing's tight, though. The party breaks up around three. Bobby ends up in Dr. M's room sometime after four, and somehow Devin times it perfectly?"

"He doesn't strike me as a criminal mastermind," Banks said.

"Maybe somebody's doing the thinking for him."

"Detective, is that a dick joke?"

"I meant Mrs. M. Mrs. Bendix. Whatever. An older woman, manipulating him."

"*Double Indemnity* meets *Sunset Boulevard*. Classic."

"You've seen *Double Indemnity,* but you've never read Poe?"

"I was raised by a black-and-white TV. You want to talk Vincent Price in *The Pit and the Pendulum,* I'm your guy. What the hell happened in Alabama?"

"Devin was caught sleeping with an underage girl—well, not underage in Alabama; she was sixteen. But the local cops arrested *her,* on charges of bestiality."

"Yikes."

"The cops dropped the charges and the case went away. No ruling from a judge on whether or not Devin was, well, a beast or a consenting human. I need to look into that—and everything else we've got on the band. We've got a shit ton of homework to do. I hate walking into these interviews blind, but every damn one of them is about to lawyer up."

"Are we going to arrest Devin?"

"We can't keep arresting WyldBoyZ, we'll get crucified. I need to find that rope. Or we get Mrs. M to admit she was covering for him. There's no way he could pull this off without her."

Luce reached the landing at the penthouse level—and nearly bumped into a man in cargo shorts. He was holding a camera with a long lens, aiming through the window in the fire door, trying to get a shot of the penthouse corridor.

"Hey!" Luce said. "This stairwell is closed!"

She gave him this: The paparazzo didn't panic. He swung his camera at her and rattled off a dozen shots.

"God damn it!" Luce said. She charged him.

The guy turned and ran down the steps, shouting, "Sorry! Leaving! Sorry!"

"What did I tell Patrol?" she said to Banks. "No fucking paparazzi!"

They marched back to the penthouse suite and Luce tore the sergeant a new asshole, which made her feel better.

Inside the suite the CSD crew were still going at it. As crime scenes went, this was an evidence-rich environment. She called over one of the techs, a white guy she'd worked with before. "After you're done, I want you to go up on the roof and photograph the flagpole."

"Uh, sure." He knew better than to fight her.

"Also, check the edges of the roof. Look for any scrape marks. Now, where's that CD player that was torn out of the wall?"

He retrieved the player, which had been sealed in a large plastic bag, along with four CDs, each in its own Baggie. Luce pulled on a pair of latex gloves.

The aluminum rails that had held the player inside its cubby were bent. The player itself was in two pieces. The five-disc tray had been pulled completely out of the machine.

Banks was looking at the four CDs without opening the bags. "*Vol. 2 . . . Hard Knock Life*," he said. "The rest are Beastie Boys, Christopher Cross, and Indigo Girls. That's some serious whiplash."

"Five-disc tray and four CDs," Luce said. She announced to the room that she was looking for CDs and if anyone found one, especially an unmarked one, to let her know.

"So what next?" Banks asked.

"It's time to interview the big guy."

"Finally! We get to talk about the elephant in the—"

"Banks!"

"You're sucking the joy out of this," he said.

"Can't Forget You"

Featuring Tusk

Tusk noticed a pair of wavering figures above the surface of the water and it gave him a start. His mind flashed on the night the barge went down—those figures on the deck, lit by flames, aiming their rifles at them. Aagh! Bad times.

He packed the memories away and surfaced. Blew water from his trunk and flapped his ears to flick the drops from them.

"It appears," Tusk said, "that I am busted."

"We did ask you to stay in your room," Detective Delgado said. She sounded amused, which was a relief.

The detectives stood a few feet back from the edge of the pool. Tusk waded toward the steps and Delgado looked away.

"Don't worry," Tusk said. "Elephants always wear trunks."

Delgado frowned, and Banks merely smiled. Typical. Matt had used the line at a party twenty-three months ago, and everyone laughed. Since then, Tusk had said the same line, word for word, four times, and his laugh rate was near zero. Humor, he thought, was the most intimate act of communication. To make a joke was to make yourself vulnerable. You were saying, Peek inside my mind. This is what I find amusing. Do you share my appreciation of it? The response could be faked, but not often, and not completely. Tusk had begun to worry that his genetic makeup put him out of sync with conventionally evolved humans. He thought he had an excellent sense of humor. Once he asked Matt if he was funny and Matt said, "No, you're hilarious." Tusk was still pondering the implications of that.

He climbed out of the pool and Delgado was kind enough to hand him his towel. He dried off, self-consciously. He knew he was extra large. Jumbo-sized, Dr. M called him. When the band appeared in person, the fans—especially the young ones, the tweeners—would swarm the others, but they would hang back from Tusk and stare up at him in some mix of fright and wonder. It was only from the distance of a stage or through a screen that he was safe enough to be loved.

"Is it time for my interview?" Tusk asked.

"We were hoping you could help us understand some things," Delgado said.

Tusk pulled on a robe. There was no one else around; the rooftop pool was in a VIP walled garden separate from the swimming area used by the IPs or the merely Ps. A perk, but also a necessity. He'd never have a moment's peace if he were forced to share the water with fans.

They took seats in the shade of a cabana. Chad—the same waiter who'd taken care of Tusk yesterday—appeared out of nowhere and glided over with a pitcher of ice water. Tusk offered to buy the detectives drinks, perhaps some food, but they declined. Tusk ordered the veggie tray.

"Great choice," the waiter said. "I'll make sure they don't skimp this time."

"Thanks, Chad," Tusk said.

"We were trying to figure out some things that happened at the party last night," Delgado said. "And Devin mentioned you have an amazing memory."

"That's a stereotype."

This made Banks smile, for some reason. The detective said, "He said you can carry an entire album in your head, every note. He says you're a genius."

"I know real geniuses. Matt, for example. I just have a head for music."

"*Matt* is a genius?" Delgado asked.

"He's brilliant. He's already been accepted to the genetics program at the University of Chicago. Even if this hadn't happened, he was quitting the band. He's going to go on and do things that change the world, I promise you."

"But you," Delgado said. "You're just the man who wrote songs that millions of people love."

She said it with kindness. He liked that she said "man."

Tusk shook his head. "I can't take credit for that. The music just comes to me."

"Ah, the I'm-just-a-vessel thing."

Tusk suddenly felt embarrassed. "Is that a cliché?"

"I've met a lot of actors and musicians," Delgado said. "It's a thing."

"But for me it's true," Tusk said. "If I have a talent, it's for producing and engineering. Figuring out how sound should best be presented for maximum effect."

"So what did you think of the CD Dr. M played last night?" Delgado asked.

The sudden swerve toward the murder unnerved him. Delgado seemed very approachable, but she was on the job, and very much in charge. Banks took his cues from her.

"I didn't think much of it," Tusk said.

Banks said, "You didn't think *much* of it? Or you didn't think much *of* it?"

"It's just a demo. Dr. M took some tape of us fooling around, from our early days. He's trying to pass it off as something new."

"But it was you," Delgado said. "The WyldBoyZ."

"We may be on the recording, but it's not the WyldBoyZ."

"You want to run that by me again?"

"If John and Paul were fooling around with a tape recorder when they were kids, you wouldn't say it was the Beatles. The WyldBoyZ is its own thing, its own sound."

The waiter placed the trays on the table. The mounds of vegetables were much bigger than the order yesterday—they were learning. "Please, have some," Tusk said. Tusk and Banks reached for the tray at the same time, but Banks suddenly froze. This was odd enough that Tusk also paused, the bundle of celery sticks still gripped in his trunk.

"On second thought," Banks said.

"You sure?" Tusk asked. "There's plenty."

"I'm good."

Tusk shrugged and popped the sticks into his mouth.

Delgado said, "So this demo Dr. M played last night. Why did he do it?"

"That was Dr. M trying to—not blackmail us, that's the wrong word—extort us into staying together. Dr. M wanted the next WyldBoyZ album, and we weren't going to give it to him. So he was threatening to release this raw, unpolished recording as our new album."

"Because Matt was leaving?" Delgado asked. "Or because of the lawsuit?"

"We all were leaving. Devin wants to be an actor, Tim wants to go hide, and frankly, I'm ready to do something else, musically. My dream is to build my own studio—my own production complex, actually. Audio, video, computer graphics, all the tools a twenty-first-century artist would need, and in a serene, isolated environment where they can create in peace."

"Sounds like you've thought about how to spend your money," Banks said.

"Money buys time and security. You can't make art if you're running for your life."

The detectives were looking at him oddly, and he realized he'd said something incriminating. "I mean from fans," he explained. "If we walk out onto the street it's like *A Hard Day's Night.*"

"Great movie," Banks said. "So why not go ahead and let Dr. M release the demo? If you're not going to make another album, make money off that."

Tusk was shaking his head before he'd finished the sentence. "Even if we were staying together, we weren't about to give Dr. M another song—not without reclaiming our rights and fixing the contract he had us sign. He's been cheating us. You don't have to take my word for it—this is all a matter of public record. You can read the complaint."

"Devin already told us Dr. M didn't write the songs," Banks said. "That it was all you and Tim."

"It's not only the copyright issue. Dr. M was paying himself as both manager and a sixth member of the band. He was double-dipping—triple-dipping if you count the songwriting credit."

"That sounds infuriating," Delgado said.

"It was. Is." Delgado was so easy to talk to. He wondered if she was trying to trap him into something.

"So this demo Dr. M played last night," she said. "I don't really understand his plan. Say he would release it as the next WyldBoyZ album. If it's from before he was your manager, he doesn't have any rights to it, does he?"

"Dr. M said if we went forward with the case, he'd argue he has *all* rights—because we're his property. Anything we produce belongs to him."

"'*I own all of you*,'" Delgado said. "That's what he said at the party."

Tusk nodded. "The matter has never been settled. In fact, Maury paid off people to make sure our status was never determined. He claims to have paperwork establishing his ownership, from our earliest days after the rescue."

"That can't hold up," Banks said. "You're obviously . . . a person."

"You'd be surprised at how difficult it is to establish personhood in America. Even if the court finds we're human, we might still be designated as illegal immigrants. We'd be . . . less than."

"No wonder," Delgado said.

"No wonder what?" Tusk asked.

"That when you heard the song, you got so angry you ripped the CD player from the wall."

Tusk chewed slowly. He hadn't realized they knew about that. Banks seemed surprised as well. Did the two detectives not confide in each other?

"I got frustrated," Tusk admitted. "I tried to stop the player, but . . ." He waggled his fingers, thick as PVC pipe. "I couldn't hit just one button. And so, yes, violence."

"Here's the thing," Delgado said. "We looked at the CD player. We can't find the CD that Dr. M was playing."

"Really? It should be . . . oh no."

The detectives waited for him to say more.

"A fan may have grabbed it," Tusk said. "It would be valuable. Not monetarily, because they wouldn't be able to release it legally. But for bragging rights. The fan community runs on a prestige economy."

"A fan," Delgado repeated. "Like the one you saw in Dr. M's room?"

"Not in the room—I saw them walking out after the party and then getting into the elevator."

That surprised them. "When was this?"

"An hour after the party ended," he said. "Four thirteen AM."

"That's an exact number," Banks said.

"I'm good with time."

"What time is it now? No peeking."

"Three thirty-two PM."

Banks looked at his watch. "You're off by a minute. It's three thirty-one."

"Your watch is slow."

"So almost twelve hours ago, at four thirteen AM, you saw the fan leave the suite," Delgado said. "This was when you were sitting in the hallway?"

"Ah, Bobby told you that? That's good—that he remembers, I mean. When he's in maximum mode, that's when he blacks out. I took Bobby back to his room a minute or two after three AM. He was drunk, high, and very . . . manic. We were used to this. On this tour especially, he's been reliably out of control. Sometimes he—is that funny?" Detective Banks had just smirked.

"I'm sorry," Banks said. "It's an oxymoron. Reliably out of control . . ."

"Oh! Yes." Tusk made a mental note: Wordplay could be funny. He should work on his wordplay.

"The hallway," Delgado prompted.

"Yes. I tried to keep Bobby inside, because he was determined to rejoin the party. Finally I shut him in—this was at three thirty—and sat outside the door, waiting for him to tire himself out. There was a lot of . . . smashing. At three forty-five, two of the hotel security staff came to investigate and I promised them he'd quiet down."

"And did he?"

"Not a bit. He went on caterwauling until after four."

"Yet the security guards didn't come back." A phone was buzzing. Delgado took a small Nokia from her pocket, looked at the screen, then put it away. "Sorry, go on. The guards?"

"Once they knew it was Bobby, they . . . well, let's just say it's one of the perks of being famous."

"And it was right around then—four thirteen, you said—that a fan walks out of the suite," Delgado said. "Can you describe them? Was it a man or a woman?"

"I couldn't tell—they were in full costume. I heard a door open, and it woke me up. I was drowsing a bit. They were walking out of the suite, heading away from me toward the elevator."

"What kind of costume?"

"Brown fur with a white stripe running down the back. A fluffy white and brown tail. Some kind of small woodland animal."

"Did anyone else see this person in the hallway?" Delgado asked. Her phone buzzed again, but she ignored it.

"There was no one else around," Tusk said. "I couldn't hear Bobby anymore, so I assumed he'd finally passed out, and I went into my room and went to sleep." Banks opened his mouth to ask a question and Tusk added, "I was in bed by four twenty." Banks closed his mouth.

"Did you see this costumed person earlier, inside the party?" Delgado asked.

"I did not. But there were a lot of people at the party, many of them in costume. Also, the suite is large, and I stayed mostly in the common area out front. Dr. M kept the door to the master bedroom closed."

"So as far you know," Delgado said, "you're the only person to have seen this costumed person."

"Ah," Tusk said. "You think I made them up."

"I didn't say that," Delgado said.

Banks said, "You have to admit it'd be really helpful to Bobby if there was somebody else in the room. And what's good for Bobby is good for the band."

"And therefore me," Tusk said.

Banks shrugged.

"You lied to us," Tusk said to Delgado.

The detective blinked in surprise. "I did?"

"You said that we weren't suspects. But of course we are."

"'Suspect' isn't a legal term," Delgado said. "But in a practical sense? Sure. Everyone in the hotel last night is a suspect."

"But especially Bobby," Tusk said. "And Tim."

Banks nearly dropped his pencil. Delgado said, "Why don't you tell me about Tim attacking Dr. M?"

"Tim is an unhappy person, but I've never seen him act out like that," Tusk said. "He's more of a seether."

"Yet he went at Dr. M and knocked him over. I'm assuming

you remember that—you were standing right there."

"Tim was angry because Dr. M was insulting Kat."

"The Queen of the Roadies," Banks said. "What's her full name?"

"Katherine Vainikolo. She's been with us almost since the beginning. She was our first bus driver, our first everything—in the early days she worked the soundboard and lights, set up the PA and tore it down, sold the merch, handled the fan mail, even combed Devin's hair. These days she manages dozens of people who do those things. The only job she can't delegate is taking care of Tim."

"What's the matter with Tim?" Banks asked.

"He's extremely shy," Tusk said. "And bitter. He's stopped talking to us, I think because he just wants all this to end. He'd quit the band if it wasn't already blowing up."

"And Kat, she's his girlfriend?"

"No!" The thought was abhorrent. "More like—I was about to say 'handler,' but that has unfortunate connotations."

"Let's say babysitter," Banks said.

Delgado looked off to the side. Tusk wondered what she was thinking about. The phone was in her hand.

"I'd like to offer my full assistance," Tusk said. "I can give you the names of everyone I saw at the party, and the descriptions of the ones I don't know."

Delgado looked up, raised an eyebrow.

"As it turns out," Tusk said, "I have a near-photographic memory."

"You said that was a stereotype," Banks said.

"It is. It just happens that in my case it's true."

Banks opened his notebook. "Let me have it."

Tusk closed his eyes. "Let's start to my left." He pictured the room as it had been at its most crowded, around 2:30 AM. "Gordon and Shweta Wisniewski were by the door, greeting people. They're a married couple. Shweta's the president of the fan club, and Gordon's her gopher. She was dressed as a zebra."

"What was Gordon dressed as?"

"I just told you."

Banks sighed, for some reason. "Go on. . . ."

"Next to them were the Dalmatian twins, Bob and Gary—"

"I'm sorry," Delgado said. Her phone was vibrating again. "You two keep going, I need to return this."

"Of course. Detective Delgado, I'm telling you the truth about seeing a person in costume leave the penthouse. And I'm serious in that I want to help you, in any way I can."

"Good to know," Delgado said.

"Skin in the Game"

Featuring Detective Delgado

Luce walked to the other side of the pool. She'd gotten five calls in the space of five minutes, and all were from the same number: her sister Maria's.

"Lo siento, no sabía que Melanie te estaba llamando," Maria said. "¡Oh!, ella está aquí mismo."

"No se la pases todavía," Luce said. Before Melanie got on the phone, she had to explain that the investigation was going to roll over onto Luce's regular night shift, so . . . could Melanie spend the night? Maria, being Maria, said it was no problem, they could even drop her off at school in the morning, wasn't a bother at all. And Luce, being Luce, promised it was the last time. None of these outrageous statements even counted as a lie. This game between the Delgado sisters had been going on so long it was like playing poker with all the cards showing.

Luce switched to English. "Okay, let me talk to Melanie."

"Mom!" Melanie shouted. "Bobby O is in jail!"

"I know, sweetness. Listen, you can't call my cell phone unless it's an emergency."

"This is an emergency! Are you investigating? Why did you

not tell me? Did he murder Dr. M?"

"We don't know yet, Mel."

"What are they like? Are they nice?"

Luce deflected those two questions, and the next thirty-two. Finally, she got to ask one of her own.

"Melanie, have you seen Bobby jump? Like, real far?"

"Oh! That's his signature move, like Tusk has the Stomp dance? In the 'Talk to the Hand' video Bobby jumped over a pickup truck, the long way! Oh my God, did you see him jump?"

"And how about Devin? Have you seen him, well, climb on things?"

"All the time, Mami. He swings across the stage, and he doesn't even use wires."

Banks walked toward Luce but stopped ten feet away, giving her some privacy. Tusk was watching them from the cabana. His trunk, seemingly moving of its own free will, found a carrot and pushed it in to his mouth.

"I'll talk to you later, mija," Luce said. "Mami's got to go look at some video herself."

———————

Las Vegas was a surveillance-happy town. In every casino, cameras nestled in the ceilings like glass wasp nests, and the gaming room in the Matador was no exception. The coverage in the hotel proper, however, was spotty. Most of the guest room hallways were on tape, but the penthouse level was a camera-free zone. No VIP wanted a video of prostitutes entering their room—at least not one that was badly filmed. There were no cameras in the stairwells, either.

The elevators, however? Each one was a tiny TV studio.

"Okay, coming up on four thirteen AM," the tech said.

Four people were jammed into the tiny video control room—the tech, Luce, Banks, and the hotel manager—all sharing the space with the manager's cologne. His name tag said: "Rudolfo." He'd recognized Luce as soon as she appeared but thankfully hadn't gone full fanboy.

"What is that?" Rudolfo asked. "A squirrel?"

"Close," Luce said.

A person in a full chipmunk costume had entered the elevator and pushed the button for the lobby with a furry hand. The head was enormous, with puffy white cheeks, huge eyes, and two pert ears on top. The fur was a rusty brown color. A thin tail, white with a dark brown streak down the middle.

In one hand the animal gripped a pillowcase that held something heavy.

"Paws!" Luce said.

The tech punched a key on the keyboard and the image froze. Also a good thing.

"Are those stains on their hands?" Luce asked.

Everyone leaned forward. "I can't tell, the color is off," the tech said. "Do you want me to go back, or . . . ?"

"Never mind. Keep rolling. And Banks, make a note to check the suite for missing pillowcases."

On-screen, the elevator doors opened and the chipmunk walked out.

"That's the elevator rotunda," Luce said. "Do we have a camera on that?"

"Just a sec," the tech said. She scrolled through a list of names like MGLOB2, pressed Return, and a video window popped up. She began reversing through the video. The chipmunk walked out of the elevator carrying the pillowcase and stepped between two mammals waiting to get on, a gorilla wearing a space helmet and a chubby fox with an enormous tail. Then the chipmunk crossed a section of the lobby. At four in the morning the space was uncrowded by Las Vegas standards, but there were a few dozen people on-screen, a third of them in costume. The chipmunk walked toward the mall—a walkway of shops and restaurants gratingly called Mercado Alley—that connected the Grand Pool, the Grand Arena, where the band had performed, and a set of Matador-owned condo towers. The tech managed to keep finding cameras with the 'munk in view—and then the suspect turned down a service hallway.

"Keep following," Luce said.

The tech worked for several seconds and said, "I'm sorry, ma'am, they don't have a camera there."

"Okay, stick with the outside of the corridor, and see if anybody comes out." No chipmunk emerged. In an hour of tape, they saw one bearded white man walk into the corridor and emerge five minutes later.

"What's in that hallway?" Banks asked.

"Restrooms," Rudolfo answered.

"Does it have an exit to the outside?" Banks asked.

"Ah! Yes! There's a fire exit."

"Show me," Luce said. To the tech she said, "Keep scanning the footage, and flag anybody who walks out of that corridor, all morning. Also, as fast as you can do it, I want pictures of the suspect from that footage. Give me all the best frames."

"Technically, there aren't really frames, there're just—"

"Do it. Jesus."

Delgado and Banks walked out of the little office, trailed

by the manager. "I want to tell you how much I admire your work," he said to Luce. "And your father's! I was a busboy at Circus Circus when you two had your show there. I was amazed! That thing you did with the swords, and you were so young! Never would I have thought I would get to work side by side with Doña Diavola. It's an honor."

"That's ancient history," she said.

"How is your father? Is he retired?"

"Extremely."

They stepped into the lobby and cameras erupted, a flurry of flashes. Luce kept her serious face on. The captain would want to give a press conference soon, with Luce by his side, and that would kill her momentum.

The lobby was more crowded than it had been when the chipmunk took their stroll. The fans stood around with their luggage, and officers were taking names and IDs.

Luce followed the chipmunk's path from the elevator to the corridor. There were three bathrooms—men, women, and family—and a door to the stairwell. At the far end was the fire exit. The sign said: EMERGENCY EXIT ALARM WILL SOUND IF DOOR IS OPENED.

"Which begs the question," Luce said.

"No one reported the alarm going off," Rudolfo said.

"Hmm," Luce said. She pushed on the crossbar. The alarm began to blare. On the other side was an open-air courtyard, populated at this moment by half a dozen smokers. The paved path was a shortcut to the VIP parking lot where she'd left her car.

She pulled it closed and the alarm stopped. "So they didn't rig the door. The alarm cuts off quick, though. We'll want to check your logs to see if anything happened your staff missed."

Rudolfo nodded once. "It will be done." He stopped just short of clicking his heels.

"Tell me about the stairwell—can you get to the other floors?"

"Only the mezzanine, just above us, and the tunnel to the parking garage, below," Rudolfo said. "The doors do not let you enter floors with the guest rooms—they're exit only, unless you have a key."

Banks was already jotting notes in his notepad. "Okay, our furry friend could have gone out through the garage tunnel, too. I'll have CSD check the cameras in the garage and outside this door."

Luce walked toward the women's restroom. "Banks, check the men's."

The restroom was large and spotless—she hoped it hadn't just been cleaned. She lifted the lid from the chrome trash can, tilted it onto its side, and shook the contents onto the floor. Nothing but paper towels. She pulled on a pair of latex gloves, then shoved her hand inside each receptacle under the sinks. Nothing. She opened each of the four stalls.

Then she went into the family restroom. One toilet, with a changing table, and a lockable door. Good for privacy. She checked the trash cans as she'd done in the other room. Then she looked up. Above the toilet, a ceiling tile was slightly out of place.

She stepped up onto the toilet. Her gloved fingers could just reach the tile. She went up on tiptoes and pushed up. A ball of fur fell out of the ceiling.

"Banks!" she called. "Banks!"

He poked his head in.

She said, "I think we have what you might call a clue."

Luce didn't unfold the costume, but she could tell that the white paws had been stained with blood—still moist. But what was more interesting was the pillowcase. Inside it were two metal contraptions. Two wristbands, each with a crossbar that fit in the palm—all the better for supporting the three metal claws. They looked handmade, like something welded out of rakes. The claws, too, were bloody.

Rudolfo was shocked. "Are these the murder weapons?"

"I dunno," Banks said. "I think we should hold out for something more on the nose."

Luce said, "Get the CSD crew in here and bag all this up. And Rudolfo—"

"Ma'am!"

"I need to talk to your security people—whoever was working last night. Evidently they had some interactions with people on the penthouse floor."

"Of course. The men are supposed to fill out incident reports for any, you know . . ."

"Incidents."

"Yes!"

"One more thing. Banks is going to bring you a list of names, guests who were at the party last night. I particularly want to talk to—what was the president's name?"

"Shweta Wisniewski," Banks said. "And her husband, Gordon."

"Right, the zebra and the gopher. If they haven't checked out yet, I'd like you to help me keep them here."

"Keep them?" Rudolfo asked. "But how?"

"Entice them. I don't know, offer them a discount in the restaurant. The LVMPD can't pay you back, but it would be a great service to the community—and we'd of course mention all your help when we catch the murderer."

The hotel manager nodded. "I have some discretionary power, Detective. I'll do my best." He hurried off.

Banks said, "So that totally screws with our case against Devin."

"It doesn't change anything."

"What?"

"Devin could fit inside that suit."

"An animal inside an animal."

"Though it's tricky," Luce said. "How does a really famous bonobo not get seen when he walks out of the restroom?"

"A second disguise! Under the chipmunk suit is, I don't know, a bear costume. That would be so great—Russian nesting mammals."

"I need to talk to Mrs. M, but she's still at the hospital. So who's left?"

"Matt and Tim."

"Well, Tim did attack Dr. M at the party. Let's start there."

"Right," Banks said. "I'm sure we can get the pangolin to come out of his shell."

"I'm not listening to you."

———

Their knock on Tim's door was answered by the small, brown-skinned woman they'd glimpsed earlier: purple hair, nose ring, and many dark tattoos marking her face and neck. She was wearing oversized gray coveralls and was yelling into a cell phone, "Well, where the fuck are they? Stack 'em by the loading dock."

Luce couldn't place her accent. It was as if Johnny Rotten

had grown up in Australia. "Just get them the fuck off the stage," the woman shouted, "or they'll fucking bill us!"

She looked at Delgado and Banks. Her eyes narrowed. Those eyes and her wide mouth were the central features in a maze of geometric tattoos: black stripes across her cheeks and down her chin, zigzags across her forehead, dots and lozenges everywhere else. The tattoos continued down her neck. The look was both animalistic and architectural.

"I gotta go," she said into the phone. "The fucking cops are here."

"You must be Kat," Luce said. "May we come in?"

The inside of the hotel room smelled deeply funky. Definitely not a human odor. The couch cushions had been moved to the floor, where they made a little fort.

"Hey, Timmy?" Kat said. "You want to come out of there? These detectives want to have a chat."

"Tell them to go away," Tim said.

"Aw, don't be like that. You're being rude."

A snout pushed through the cushions.

"There's a good boy," Kat said.

The rest of him emerged. Luce had seen pictures of Timmy P and had watched him on TV, but it was a shock to meet him in person; he was definitely the most purely animal of the bunch. He looked exactly like a pangolin—which meant that he looked a lot like an armadillo, though one wearing a T-shirt and jeans. He was all curled up, but she doubted he was over four feet tall if he stood up on those clawed feet—and a good portion of his body length was due to the long, flat tail that jutted from a seam at the back of those jeans, and spooned around him. The tail was plated in overlapping gray scales, and his head and arms were covered in the same armor. His hands ended in long, curving claws. More than Bobby, or anyone else in the band, he had the natural weapons to carve Dr. M into pieces.

Tim blinked at her from beady eyes set far back behind his long snout. His tiny mouth frowned.

"Hi, Tim. My name's Detective Delgado, and this is—"

"Nope." Tim pushed back under the cushions.

"Tim!" Kat said.

He didn't answer.

Kat sighed. "Just a sec. I have an idea."

Track 9

"You Don't Know Pop"

Featuring Timmy P

Tim had been dreading this moment. All morning he'd lain curled in the dark, quietly freaking the hell out. What was going to happen to Bobby O? If they freed Bobby, would they accuse Tim? Kat? Someone else in the band? What if they made everybody stay in this hotel and he never got to burrow? In times like these—and almost all times were like these, though admittedly, violent homicide was a fresh wrinkle—nothing chilled him out more than a good excavation session.

He'd gone to his backup stress management technique: contemplating future dooms. For years after escaping the barge he imagined all the ways the CIA could abduct the band and subject them to medical experiments, but when the government failed to materialize, that particular dread lost its sting. Most of last year he'd soothed himself with thoughts of Y2K, and it was a big disappointment when the digital apocalypse evaporated in January. Climate change was an up-and-comer, and planet-killing asteroids were good for a quick, comforting jolt. But when all other dooms failed, he contemplated the terror of Shell Cancer.

Shell Cancer had not yet been discovered, as far as he knew. But the problem with being a genetic one-off was that no one, absolutely no one, could tell you what pangolin-human-hybrid diseases and disorders were likely, and which predispositions to them were waiting in his genome. If there were a significant population of PHHs who'd been living on the planet for a couple hundred years and, even better, a community of American PHHs who'd immigrated in the 1800s to, say, Pittsburgh, attracted by the region's many mining opportunities, and had turned its famous "Pangotown" into a vibrant community noted for its underground homes and termite restaurants, and who, despite having fallen on hard times when the steel industry collapsed in the 1970s, had nevertheless persevered and found work in the nascent knowledge economy thanks in part to the species' obsessive focus, work ethic, and a tendency toward nearsightedness that made them perfect for screen work, why, if *that* had happened then there would be statistics on the rate of Shell Cancer, epidemiologists charting its spread, and teams of smart, highly educated *Homo*-pangolins working on a cure, or at least a treatment cream.

He heard rustling outside his cushions, and then Kat said, "I brought you breakfast."

A tangy smell made its way through the gap.

"Come on now," Kat said, her voice growing firm. "These detectives don't have all day. Besides, you don't want me to throw out fresh grub."

Tim eased his snout back into the room. "Grubs?"

Kat extended her free hand. "Up and out, there you go."

"This won't take long," Detective Delgado said.

Tim sat on the floor with the bag of snacks between his knees. Kat handed him his glasses and the sinister blurs resolved into a Hispanic woman and thirtyish white man whose head would soon be as hairless as Tim's. He introduced himself as Detective Banks.

"I didn't do it," Tim said. Then immediately regretted it. Nothing made you sound guiltier than instantly denying it. "Bobby didn't, either," he added.

"Everybody seems to agree on that," Detective Banks said. He pulled out a tape recorder. "You mind if I—oh God."

"You missed one, love," Kat said. She pointed to the corner of her mouth. "Right here." Tim used his foreclaw to push the white beetle larva between his lips.

"Can you tell me where you two were last night, from the time you left the party, till this morning?"

"I was here," Tim said.

"That's the truth," Kat said. "He got under the cushions as soon as we got in, and hasn't moved since."

"And you?" Banks asked her.

"I took the bed. I was here until seven thirty or so. I took the elevator down and walked over to the venue to start on the teardown. Oh, stopped at the Starbucks to get coffee for my crew. Then I got a call from Matt saying Dr. M was dead, the cops were coming, and Tim wouldn't come out."

"Sorry," Tim said quietly.

"It seems like you've been having a rough time," Delgado said.

"What do you mean?" he asked.

"We heard that you attacked Dr. M last night," Delgado said.

"Because Dr. M was being an asshole!"

"My knight in keratin armor," Kat said. To the detectives she said, "If you're thinking of accusing Tim of anything, forget it. I've already called the record company, and they're sending a pack of lawyers. And they won't be locals, like that guy they rushed over to help Bobby O."

"We're just trying to find out what happened," Delgado said. "Some of you are already helping us. Tusk is being super helpful."

"He is?" Tim said.

"Bobby's the obvious suspect—he was there at the scene of the crime. But it may not be him. In fact, for my daughter's sake, I really hope it's not him, or any of you."

"You have a daughter?" Kat asked. "How old?"

"She's nine. Huge fan." To Tim she said, "Just this morning, she was singing 'Deep Down' at the top of her lungs. She loves your songs."

"I've written a lot of songs," Tim said sadly. "But that's the one they always bring up first."

"Your words go so well with the music. The music's so simple and singable, and your words—"

"What did you say? *Simple?*"

"I didn't mean anything by it, just that my daughter—"

"Say what you want about my lyrics, but do *not* talk about the music that way. You don't know what the hell you're talking about."

"I'm sure I don't, but—"

"Listen to me! Your average pop song has eight, maybe nine unique sounds—bass, guitar, drums, some synth, and a singer with maybe some backing vocals. And your average *boy band* adds five voices that need to be in every damn song, and that muscles out the other sounds. They put a lead singer in the middle, put everybody else on three-five interval harmonies, and call it a day.

"But WyldBoyZ songs? You have no idea. We have all

sorts of instrumentals, sometimes ten distinct sounds at once, *plus* our vocals, all without overlapping frequencies! Drum machines, percussion samples, synth sounds, real instruments—that guitar on 'One of a Kind' isn't a patch, that's a real lap steel guitar. Just by production value, our songs are more authentic and varied than anything anyone else is putting out. And I haven't even gotten to the singing!"

Tim realized he'd risen to his feet, and his toe claws were digging into the carpet. He didn't fucking care.

"Devin thinks it's all about the lead singer, but we put two singers on counterpoint with harmonies, and full group harmonies on the choruses, and it *works*. Do you think it's *easy* to balance our five voices? Tusk sounds like he's inside a barrel, and Matt blows out our high frequencies—it's a nightmare in the studio. Then there's all the interplay. We do these crazy starts and stops on syncopated rhythms, and if any one of us messes that up live, it all falls apart. We're performing songs with no room for error—while we're *dancing*.

"Think about that chorus in 'Home'—you ever hear a hard right turn like that in another pop song? One moment we're singing about loneliness and longing, and then *bam*, a full-on dance beat for sixteen bars, then back to the ballad! People like you hear that and think, oh, it's a joke, it's *sloppy*. No. No way. Twenty years from now some young musician will put on that track, hear that change, and it will *blow* their *minds*.

"Oh, but let's talk about the *simple* one, 'Deep Down,' everybody's goddamn favorite. You know the two gaps before the choruses? We end on a nonfunctional harmony and then go to total silence. That leaves the listener totally high and dry for a full *two seconds* before the chorus hits. That's forever in pop music! Fans say it gives them chills, right, because of our beautiful voices or whatever, but really it's because it was written to make them *need* the resolution, and then withholds it! You ever hear a whole stadium of teenage girls go dead quiet in the middle of a pop concert? That's us. That's what we do."

The detectives were staring at him, openmouthed. Kat wore a sad smile.

Tim thought, Oops, I did it again.

The fury left his body. He sat down, looked at the empty grub bag. "Anyway. It's not simple."

"I apologize," Detective Delgado said gently. "I have to admit, I haven't paid close attention to your music, but I'm sure my daughter has. She's already more of a musician than I am."

"Go on," Tim said. "Ask your questions."

"I was just wondering if it was possible you lost control a bit when you argued with Dr. M."

"I may have scratched him," Tim said.

"Tim . . . ," Kat said in a warning voice.

"It's okay," he said to her. "I can do this." He took off his glasses and rubbed them on his shirt. "What do you want to know?"

"Did you break the skin?"

"I don't know. I know I tore his shirt."

"When you got back to the room did you notice any blood on . . . yourself?"

"You can just say claws," Tim said. "And no."

"Have you ever fought with Dr. M before? Physically or verbally?"

"I don't say much to him. I mean, I didn't."

"But you didn't like him."

"Nobody liked him," Tim said. "He's a hybrid, too—ten

percent human, ninety percent scumbag. He was conning us from the beginning."

"Let's talk about the beginning, then," Delgado said. "How did you meet Dr. M?"

"He wasn't Dr. M when I met him," Tim said.

———————

And the boys weren't the WyldBoyZ. They were refugees. Monster refugees.

Tim told the detectives how the five of them had spent more than two weeks crammed together on the lifeboat, lost in the Pacific, no help in sight. They were all exhausted, Tusk especially. The motor wouldn't start, so Tusk had pulled them away from the burning barge using a line looped around his neck, paddling and paddling, mostly submerged with only his trunk above the water. For the first two days he spent hours in the water, pulling them east, toward South America. That stopped when the sharks arrived. From that point on, the boys spent most of the day under a tarp, out of the harsh sun. Matt's skin was cracking, Devin's hair was falling out in clumps, and even Bobby had stopped talking. And what did Tim do to help them? Nothing. He spent all his time, day and night, curled into a ball. A coward.

Tusk made sure they rationed the water, which lasted until Day Fifteen. On Day Seventeen, an Ecuadoran fishing boat spotted them. The crew took one look at them and refused to allow them on board. They thought the animals would attack. But they did lower a bucket of water and a bag of cat food. That's when Devin stood up and, in his dehydration-cracked voice, began swearing at them. The crew didn't have a lot of

English, but they knew the essentials, such as "goddamn" and "motherfuckers." The crew laughed uproariously. They never allowed the boys onto their boat, but the food got better.

The fishermen towed them east for two days and cut them loose at Isla Isabella. "Oh my God," Matt had said. "We're in the Galápagos Islands. This is where Darwin figured out evolution."

"Why are you laughing?" Tim asked.

"Because a hundred years ago, we could have fucked his shit *up*."

The Galápagos, as far as Tim was concerned, were hell. The newspeople had found them, and the boys were harassed every waking minute and many of the sleeping ones. A hotel was putting them up for free and let them eat in the restaurant as long as they allowed tourists to photograph them. On the third day the foreign press descended, and soon the boys were on BBC, and then CNN and National Geographic. The boys knew most of the news personalities; they'd had not much to do on the barge except watch television, and most of television was American.

The boys were on a satellite feed with Katie Couric, America's Sweetheart, when they accidentally changed their lives. Katie asked them how they kept their spirits up while they were imprisoned on the ship, and Bobby said, "Whenever I'm feeling sad, I simply remember my favorite things."

"You mean like the song?"

"How did you know? Singing is our favorite thing!"

Then Katie asked them to sing something. Of course it came out in five-part harmony, because that's the way they'd learned every song.

The next morning, a large, very sweaty man sat down at

their table. The tourists never did this—they took tons of pictures but always stayed well back, as if the boys might at any moment charge and tear out their throats. The intruder smiled broadly and extended a hand to each of them. "I'm Maury Bendix," he said. "And I'm going to make you rich and famous."

Tim groaned. Tusk said, "We don't want to be famous."

"We don't?" Devin said.

"How about rich?" Bobby asked.

"Fuck off, Maury Bendix," Matt said in a cheery voice.

"Hear me out," Maury said. He took a napkin from Tim's place setting and mopped his brow. "Jesus Christ, is it humid here."

"Please leave the table," Tusk said. He'd lost weight during the two weeks at sea, but he was still formidable.

"Let me ask you a question," Maury said. "What are you going to do when the CIA comes for you?"

"Why would the CIA come for us?" Tusk asked. But Tim had already been worried about just such an eventuality.

"There's no one else like you," Maury said. "You're crazy genetic mix-'em-ups! I heard your story, that whole thing about growing up on some fucking secret science barge run by evil scientists and whatnot. There's not more of you, right? No more on the boat?"

Tim winced. Tusk said, "No. Not anymore."

"Which goes to my point—you're unique! You think the other governments don't want to get a hand on you? Take you apart to see how you work?"

"That's what I've been saying," Tim said.

"Listen to the armadillo," Maury said. "It's a rough world out there. The only way to protect yourself—the *only* way—is to be so famous and so rich that they can't touch you. You have to be beloved, and right fucking now!"

"Beloved sounds good," Devin asked. "How do we do that?"

"I manage bands. Music groups. You can become the biggest thing the world's ever seen, just by using your God-given talents."

"I don't think God gave us those," Matt said.

Maury ignored him. "We gotta get you a name—I've been working on some ideas on the plane. What do you think of Doctor Darwin and the Zoo Crew? I'm just spitballin', the name is flexible. But we really gotta decide your personas. You, cat boy, you're obviously the cute one, I want to hug you right now. Who's the funny one?"

"Personas?" Tusk asked.

"Okay, we'll figure the rest of you out on the flight back," Maury said. "The key thing is to nail down the marketing message before the first press conference on dry land."

"You can fly us to the United States?" Tusk asked.

"Of course! I'm your manager! They're going to love you, it's going to be like the Beatles landing at Kennedy. Nobody's really famous until they're famous in America."

"Like King Kong," Matt said.

"Exactly! Now here's the thing—do you have any original songs? Anything we can work with?"

Everyone looked at Tusk.

"We may have one or two recordings."

"Fantastic! Let's hear 'em."

Maury loved the music, but the flight never happened. He didn't know who to bribe to get them Ecuadoran passports, and because the boys had no ID and their legal status was highly questionable, US passports were out of the question. They sat in that hotel for three weeks while Maury called embassies, arranged interviews, and sent pleading emails to record companies. Unfortunately, no one could think of a band name that met Maury's three criteria: It had to sound exciting to ten-year-old girls, it had to hit the animal theme, and it had to be an unused trademark.

"I won't do it," Devin said sometime at the start of Week Four. "I won't be a part of any band that has an animal in the name."

"Right," Matt said. "We're not the Beatles. Or the Beastie Boys. Or the Animals."

Tim lay curled up under the coffee table. He was so tired of the talking.

Tusk said, "What's the top one on our list?"

Paper rustled. Bobby said, "Boys 2 Animals."

"That'll get us sued," Matt said.

"And it's not scientifically accurate," Tusk said. "We didn't start as boys. Our genetic structure—"

"This is demeaning," Devin said. "It's not our genetic structure that sets us apart, it's our singing. Our harmonies. Who we are in our souls. Names don't matter."

"Devin's right. We shouldn't even have a name—people should just know."

"Fuck you, Matt."

"It'll be like the Black Album," Matt said.

"You mean the White Album," Tusk said.

"Nope."

"We're not animals or humans," Devin said. "We're all things! Animal, human, white, Black . . ."

"Wait, are we white or Black?" Bobby asked.

"Race is a construct," Tusk said.

"You mean like a robot?"

"Yes, Bobby," Matt said. "Race is a robot."

"That's what I'm talking about," Devin said earnestly. "Who's more constructed than we are? We're all races, and we are all—"

"I don't see color," Matt said.

"Bullshit," Devin said.

"Literally, I don't see color."

"Tim, what do you think? Tim? Helloooo."

"Please don't knock on my shell, Bobby."

"Give us an idea for a name. I was thinking Furr-Evah. Two r's and an 'evaaaah.'"

Devin groaned.

"Two of us don't have fur," Tusk said.

"It's a metaphor!" Bobby said.

"The name doesn't matter," Tim said. "None of this matters."

Tusk said, "In some ways the name *doesn't* matter. The Beach Boys didn't surf, and yet—"

"How about *Souls*?" Devin said. "No! *The Naked Souls*."

"—their music transcended labels and content. Mozart by any other name would still be Mozart."

"That was his stage name," Matt said. "He was born Amadeus Buttlicker."

"*I do not lick my butt!*" Bobby shouted.

"Dude," Devin said. "We've all seen it."

Maury had stepped into the room. "Boys! Listen up! We have a plan—I figured out how to get you across the border. Plus! We have a bus and we're driving to the US of A. This is our driver."

No one spoke for five seconds.

Now Tim was curious. He slowly unrolled, and the clacking

noise seemed to fill the room. A short, tattooed woman in blue coveralls stood next to Maury. Tim raised his hand and said, "Hi."

"What do you know," the woman said. "A talking pangolin."

"And that's how we came to America," Tim said.

"Typical immigrant story," Kat said. Detective Banks laughed. She said, "They changed their band name a dozen times during the bus ride. I made the mistake of mentioning the Moreau novel, and that was the one thing Maury wouldn't let go of."

"The last adaptation was terrible," Banks said. "Forget Val Kilmer—give me Burt Lancaster or Charles Laughton any day."

"How did Dr. M get you across the border?" Delgado asked.

"This is embarrassing," Tim said.

"Exotic animal license," Kat said. "They came as property. Also a typical immigrant story."

"It caused a lot of problems, later," Tim said. "The contract we signed with Maury was not enforceable, because we weren't considered human beings. It wasn't until the Alabama thing that this all came out."

"The bestiality case against Devin?" Banks asked.

"Everything was evidence," Tim said. "The contracts, the animal license, the shipping invoices. The DA found everything."

Detective Delgado said, "And that's when you realized Dr. M was ripping you off?"

"Right. But suddenly he had to testify that he'd misled the

US government, or else Devin would be declared an animal—"

"You'd all be declared animals," Kat said.

"And then the band would be over. So then he had to pay us according to the contract."

"And even that contract was fucking egregious," Kat added, "I told the boyz so. Yes, they got millions, but there's millions more that Maury was hiding. I told them they ought to sue."

"Did Dr. M suspect you'd been helping the band?" Banks asked her.

"Oh yeah, he knew at the end. I didn't fucking care. I'm exhausted. I've spent seven years on a bus with a bunch of bickering teenagers. Forget everything else, just imagine the *smells*."

Tim already knew she felt this way, but it still hurt to hear. Kat noticed him cringing. "Aw, Timmy, you know I love the band. But I'm ready to move on."

"That's too bad," Delgado said. "It seems like you've been the glue holding them together. Tusk says you've done almost every job for them, down to sorting the mail."

"Ah fuck. I suppose I have. No wonder I'm tired."

"Did Dr. M receive any hate mail? Anything from someone who might wish him harm? Threats, email . . ."

"Only every fucking day," Kat said. "Mostly from what Dr. M called backstreet bitches."

"What now?" Banks asked.

"Sorry—his name for fans of other bands. Dr. M did an interview where he cast aspersions on some of the competition, and since then he's been a target. Stupid thing to do, no percentage in it, but that's the way he was."

"Any of this mail stand out?" Delgado asked.

"Like, 'I'm going to dress up and murder you in bed'? We have a team of people handling the mail now, but any specific and credible threat we flag for the lawyers at our label, and they alert the police if they feel the need. I can give you the numbers of the people who handle that shit."

"Now would be good," Delgado said. She picked up something from the carpet with two fingers and dropped it into a bag. "You mind if I use your bathroom for a second? I want to wash my hands."

"Right around there," Tim said.

Delgado went around the corner and a few seconds later shut the bathroom door. Kat found the first name in her contacts and read off the number to Banks. Tim began to feel uncomfortable with all these strangers in his room. He thought, Maybe I could slowly ease back behind these cushions. . . .

Delgado came back out. "Thanks for that. I'll try to leave you alone—you look as tired as I am. How'd you sleep last night?"

"Me?" Tim said. "Fine. I mean, the same. I've only had a few good nights since this tour started."

"I know what you mean," Delgado said. "I work nights and I have trouble. A kid at home, daytime noise, all that. I use a sleep mask and earplugs sometimes. I was thinking, maybe I need to make myself a cave out of couch cushions."

"It's a poor substitute," Tim said.

"For what?" she asked.

"A real cave," Tim said. That should have been obvious. "Or at least a good hole. When we were recording the first album, we were staying at Dr. M's house and he let me dig in his backyard. There's nothing better than a cool, dark burrow."

"But you didn't have that growing up, I'm guessing. Being on a boat."

"They kept us in cages," Tim said. "During the day we had the lounge container, and the exercise container. No dirt anywhere."

"What do you mean by 'containers'? Like, a container ship?"

"Exactly." Had she not read any of the press material? "Every metal container was a room, and lots of them were welded together, with hatches between them. Three containers were the common room, and that's where we spent most of our time when we weren't locked in our cells. There was a TV, a boombox, boxes of VHS tapes and CDs and paperbacks. The staff brought that stuff on board and let us have it when they were done. They thought it was amazing when we learned to read. Then Tusk learned how to play this Casio keyboard—it was a toy, really, but he could hit the keys by holding pencils. They thought that was amazing, too."

"And one night, this giant ship just . . . sank?"

Everyone's eyes were on him. Even Kat had looked up from her phone.

"We never found out what happened," Tim said. "There was an explosion, lots of people running around. Someone unlocked the cages, and the five of us got to the lifeboat."

"Just the five of you?"

"What?"

"Just the five of you," Delgado repeated. "No other staff, no other . . . prisoners? Dr. M asked you the same thing, you said."

"Just us five."

"But there were people on board you cared for. Is that who Sofia was?"

Tim felt his chest tighten. "How do you . . . ? Oh. Right. I'm stupid."

"My daughter sings 'Deep Down,' all the time," she said. "There's a line about Sofia, when you're in prison."

"I know the lyrics," Tim said. He remembered the night he wrote them.

> *That night behind my prison bars*
> *I heard you singing to the moon and stars.*
> *Oh, Sofia, did you know what they'd do?*
> *I can't believe that they would go that far.*

"I had to pick a girl's name," he said. "And I liked Sofia because of the pun." He looked up into the detectives' blank faces. "Sofia means 'knowledge,' so saying, 'did you know' right after is . . . clever? At least I thought so. No one cares about that kind of thing, not in a pop song, but it makes me happy."

"But Sofia's based on a real person," Delgado said.

"I don't want to talk about it."

"You don't have to," Kat said. Delgado objected and Kat added, "We can wait on the lawyers for the rest of it."

Tim shoved himself back between the cushions. One fell over, and Kat helpfully placed it over him. He listened to them as Kat gave them the second name she'd been looking up—the record label lawyer who processed the hate mail. They also asked her for the names of anyone in her crew who was at the party last night, and she gave them half a dozen names, mostly publicity people. The techies held their own parties, in their own hotel.

"I can still hear you," Tim said, loudly.

"I'm sorry we bothered you," Delgado said. Her voice was

close; she was leaning down toward the cushions. "I know this is a really stressful time."

Tim leaned so that he could see through the gap between the cushions. He looked Delgado in the eye. "You think this is stressful?" he said. "This is nothing compared to Shell Cancer."

Track 10

"Beast Folk"

Featuring Detective Delgado

Kat ushered them out and in the hallway closed the door behind her. "Sorry about that," she said quietly. "Those boys got fucked, growing up like they did. Major PTSD, and Tim's got it worse than the others."

"Sure, sure," Luce said. Her pulse had ticked up a few notches because of something she'd seen in the room, but she kept her face and voice calm.

"Do you know what happened to this Sofia?" Banks asked.

"I don't even know her real name, just that whatever happened on that barge, it broke Tim's heart. All of 'em, really, and they haven't dealt with it. I mean, Bobby drinks too much, Tim's a basket case, Matt pretends like he doesn't have feelings. . . ."

"What about Tusk?" Luce asked.

"Ha! Tusk doesn't *know* he has feelings. But he does. I hope they get into fucking therapy after all this. Well, someone besides the quack that Devin's seeing. Maybe then they'll forgive each other."

"What do you mean?"

"They've been fighting nonstop for months. Everyone's pissed at Devin, Devin resents Tusk, Tim's stopped talking to everybody but me. Tusk and Matt get along, but Matt's had one foot out the door for a while now."

"And Bobby?" Luce asked.

"Everybody likes Bobby," she says. "And everybody hates him. He's annoying as fuck. Don't tell that to your daughter."

"There's so much I can't tell her. It's going to be bad enough when she finds out the band's breaking up. She's not just a fan—she wants to *be* them. She's been performing in choirs, and she's already started writing her own songs."

"Really? Good for her."

"Magician, musician," Banks said. "It's all showbiz."

Kat looked quizzical and Banks said, "Detective Delgado here had a magic act, back in the day. Her and her father. Played some big rooms on the Strip."

Luce shot him a look.

Kat said, "Can you show me a trick?"

"No," Luce said. "Does Dr. M have a laptop?"

The conversational curveball seemed to throw Kat for a second. "It's an old black ThinkPad," she said. "It should be in his room. Is it missing?"

"I'm sure it'll turn up," Luce said. "Do you know if it's password protected?"

"Oh yeah," Kat said. "Maury kept his accounts on there, and he was fucking paranoid about financial data."

"Understandable, considering he was being sued." She took a breath. "I think that's it for now. Could I ask a personal question, though?"

Kat's eyes narrowed. "That depends."

"How many months?"

"Aw fuck, you can tell?"

"I figure last trimester. The coveralls are hiding it pretty well."

"Don't tell the boyz—they'll stop listening to me. I just want to get them taken care of, before I go settle down and leave this shit behind."

"Sounds like a good idea. Seems like you've been through enough."

Kat frowned, then seemed to come to a decision. "You seem like a nice person, so fair warning? I booked a jet to fly the boyz back to Orlando in the morning. We all want to help, but we're walking out of here at nine sharp. The lawyers have already talked to your sheriff, and they say you're not going to go to the wall for this material witness bullshit."

"What the hell?" Luce said.

"Word is, Bobby's not even your top suspect anymore."

———

Luce didn't explode with anger—immediately.

She walked past the cops guarding the penthouse suite door, went into the suite's first bathroom, shut the door, and screamed into a towel.

She left the bathroom feeling only fractionally better. Banks watched her, afraid to speak, and finally said, "I shouldn't have brought up the magic act."

"No, you shouldn't have." She got out her Nokia and dialed Captain DeAndrea, her immediate supervisor.

"Hey there, Captain," she said, with razor cheeriness. "You want to tell me why all my witnesses are being allowed to flee the state tomorrow?"

"Because tomorrow they won't be yours," the captain said. "Federal agents will be here in the morning."

"No, this case is my baby."

"It's *our* baby, for one special night. It's like foster care. Besides, you've got a prime suspect on video who's not the cat man we're holding."

"All we've got is a costume," Luce said. "We don't have a photo of the person inside it."

"Is Bobby O still a suspect?" the captain asked.

"No."

"Are you ready to charge any of the other animals?"

"That's rude. And no."

"Then this is what's going to happen. I'll be releasing Bobby O and announcing we have a new suspect—a costumed killer—and we're in pursuit. And we're going to do both those things tonight, before the WyldBoyZ sue us and the feds grab all the glory."

Luce wanted to throw the phone off the balcony, but it was expensive.

"Fifteen hours?" Banks asked. "That's not fair. In any decent movie, the hard-ass captain gives the detectives twenty-four hours to solve the case. Eddie Murphy got forty-eight."

"Eddie's the criminal in that movie," Luce said.

"Are you saying you'd rather be Nick Nolte? Nobody wants to be Nick Nolte, except for Gary Busey. Lionel! Who would you rather be?"

The mustachioed Lionel Paget had appeared from the back bedroom, lugging his crime scene bag. "Kris Kristofferson."

"You get everything?" Luce asked.

"I got a lot," Lionel said. "But not near enough. By all indications there was a hundred people traipsing through here last night. You wouldn't believe the hair clog we found in the hot tub drain."

"You didn't happen to find a laptop, did you? A black IBM?"

"No, ma'am. But I do have this for you." He handed her a folder. "All the stills from the video. Sorry they're smeary—we used the ink-jet they had in the office center. I'll have good ones made back at the office."

"You're the best, Lionel. Don't fill up your dance card to-morrow, though. I may be calling with some extra credit."

"Is that so?"

"We'll see. And of course I'd like to see the pictures soon as you get them."

"They're all digital—I'll have them on the server soon as we get back."

Luce sat down in the middle of the huge couch. God, she was tired. "I've made a huge mistake," she said. "Two mistakes. Both come from being too nice to celebrities. I should have kicked all of them out of their rooms, turned the whole floor upside down. But I worried if I got them moving, they'd scatter."

"You're doing that Great Detective thing," Banks said. "You know something, but you're not sharing it with the idiot assistant. I just want to say, it's not my fault I didn't see she was pregnant. I've been taught never to comment on a woman's weight."

"That's a good rule."

"So what's with the laptop? I didn't know Dr. M had a computer, let alone that we were supposed to be looking for it."

"It's been on my mind since Bobby told us about the party. I don't know what happened to it."

"Maybe the chipmunk stole it."

"That would be stupid of them—find it on them and it'd be

pretty easy to tie it to Dr. M. And now they're stuck trying to break his password."

"Maybe they're a hacker," Banks said. He frowned, making his entire forehead wrinkle.

"What is it?" Luce asked.

"Chipmunk hackers. There's a pun there, I can feel it."

"I have faith in you."

"So what's the second thing?" Banks asked. "You said you made two mistakes."

"I should have moved Tim out of his room."

"Why?"

"You didn't see it?" Luce asked. "In the hallway leading to the bathroom, there was blood on the carpet. A few drops, and a few more right next to the bathroom door. It may not even be blood, but I took a sample, and swabbed the sink." She'd thought about giving the evidence to Lionel, but then she'd have to explain why she didn't have his team do it. Better to get forgiveness later.

"Wait," Banks said. "So Tim did draw blood?"

"I don't know. But now I want to see if they do anything about it. If they go out for cleaning supplies, that'll tell us something."

"Entrapment!" Banks said. "I love it. I'll call down to Rudolfo and cancel maid service, then ask the boys out front to watch Tim's door."

"Do it quick." She glanced at her watch. How the hell was it already 6:00 PM? She was exhausted and starving. If she didn't eat soon a headache would kick in. At least Melanie was getting fed; she never failed to remind her mother that Aunt Maria was a better cook than her. Which was unfair. You can't be declared bad at something you'd never attempted.

She rested her head back on the couch and stared at the ceiling. The balcony door had been closed long enough and the air conditioning had caught up. Room temperature was back to Las Vegas Standard, aka Casino Cold.

Banks returned. "I've got some news—Gordon and Shweta Wisniewski, the fan club people, are waiting to talk to us. They're about to catch a shuttle to the airport."

"Shit. Okay." Luce held out an arm, and Banks pulled her upright.

They walked the short distance to the elevator and pressed the button. Suddenly Banks stood straight and made a surprised noise.

"What is it?" she asked.

He turned to her, his eyes lit up. "Silicon Chip 'n' Dale."

The only clues that they were talking to a zebra and a gopher were the tails clipped to their belt loops. Shweta's was a long striped braid ending in a black pouf. Gordon's was brown and fluffy. Gordon saw Luce looking at it and said, "I know, it's not anatomically correct, gopher tails are, well, kind of ratlike, but Shweta—"

"I like it, honey." The couple were holding hands, and she raised his hand and kissed it. "It's sexy."

Shweta Wisniewski was a short East Indian woman whose hair was cut in a bob, Gordon a round-faced white man. Travel wear consisted of cargo shorts, Sun Microsystems polos, and white Reeboks—for both of them.

"Please, have a seat," Luce said. Rudolfo had lent them a conference room.

"We don't have long," Shweta said apologetically. "We're flying back to Columbus today and the shuttle leaves in a half hour."

"When's your flight leave?" Banks asked.

Gordon checked his digital watch. "Three hours and twenty minutes."

"We like to be early," Shweta said.

Luce suppressed a groan. They could have done this an hour from now—after interviewing Matt, after getting dinner. But now that they were here, there was no way out but through.

"We don't mind being a little late," Gordon said. "We want to help. Bobby couldn't have done this, and if there's any way we can help clear his name, we'll do it."

Banks opened his notebook. "You were at the party last night, yes?"

"We like to work the door, as they say," Shweta said.

"So many people try to get in, and not the right people," Gordon added. "Sometimes, um, professional ladies?"

"Got it," Banks said. "So you would have seen everybody who came in and tried to get in—zoomies, crew members, prostitutes—"

"You . . . Oh. Wow. I wish you wouldn't use that word."

"'Prostitutes'?"

"'Zoomies,'" Gordon said. "The proper term is 'zoomandos.' We're adult fans of the WyldBoyZ, separate from kidfans, but also distinct from furry fandom in general. Though you don't have to wear a fursuit to be a zoomando—"

"Not in the least!" Shweta added.

Banks said, "And 'zoomie' is . . . ?"

"Offensive," Shweta said. "Deeply offensive."

"Well . . . ," Gordon said.

"Most of the time," Shweta said. "We're allowed to use it amongst ourselves, especially if you're an LTZ, otherwise, you should really avoid it."

Luce sighed.

"No idea," Banks said to her. Then to Shweta: "LTZ?"

"Long Term Zoomando."

"Of course," Banks said.

"Like Shweta and I," Gordon said. "We were there from the beginning. We met at a Wylding. I looked across the room, and there she was, being spit roasted by the Dalmatian twins. We made eye contact and bing! Magic."

"So this is a sex thing," Banks said.

"My God, that's so . . ." Shweta put up a hand. "That's not part of it at all."

"Well, it's a part of it," Gordon said.

"But it doesn't define us," Shweta said. "Do we have sex to-gether? Yes, just like everyone else. Do we keep our fursuits on while we do it? Sometimes! And do we find it freeing to em-brace a part of ourselves that society—"

"Thanks for that," Luce said. She pushed a photo at them. "Do you remember seeing this person at the party?"

Shweta and Gordon peered at the picture of the chipmunk leaving the elevator.

"Nope, they weren't there," Shweta said. "We'd remember."

"*Oh* yeah," Gordon said.

"It's not one of your zoomandos?" Luce asked.

"Definitely not," Shweta said. "None of our people would be caught dead in that."

Gordon was shaking his head. "It's store-bought."

"You can tell that from this picture?" Banks asked.

"That's some knock-off of a knock-off. See how baggy it is? There's no craft there. No customization. You'd just buy that off the rack in a Halloween store."

"All right, fine," Luce said. "Can you tell us who you do remember?"

Banks opened his notebook to the page of names he'd taken from Tusk, placing a checkmark next to each name the Wisniewskis confirmed and adding new ones.

After they'd finished Banks asked them about everything they remembered and they confirmed much of what Bobby, Devin, and Tusk had told them. They saw Bobby hanging over the pool table, watched in alarm as Tim knocked down Dr. M. Saw Devin and Mrs. M come out from the Jacuzzi.

"It broke up pretty quickly after that," Shweta said. "Which was sad, it being the last party and all."

"The WyldBoyZ may never sing together again!" Gordon said.

"You heard they're breaking up?" Delgado asked.

"Everybody knows the boyz are suing Dr. M and he's counter-suing," Shweta said. "Dr. M won't give in, and it'll be ugly."

"So the fans blame Dr. M?" Delgado asked.

"Of course! He didn't write the songs!"

"So the party broke up early," Banks said. "What time did you leave?"

"Oh, this must have been just after three," Shweta answered. "We were the last to leave."

"Except for Matt, and Dr. M," Gordon said.

"Matt stayed behind?" Luce asked.

"Just for a few minutes," Shweta said. "We were waiting to get on the elevator—there was a bit of a traffic jam and the hotel security guards were trying to get everyone to leave the floor. I was just a few feet from the penthouse door. I heard Dr. M shouting, then the door banged open, and Matt walked out, looking upset. Matt's never upset, he's always . . . not cheerful, like Bobby, but funny in a kind of cynical way, sort of—"

"Bemused?" Gordon said.

"Sardonic," Shweta said.

"Can you tell us what they were arguing about?" Luce asked.

"I don't know," Shweta said. "But when Matt walked out, Dr. M yelled, 'You think I won't tell the effing world about you freaks?' *That* got Matt angry."

"Really angry," Gordon said.

"That's the exact wording?" Luce asked.

"Well, he didn't say 'effing,'" Gordon said. "It was the other word. But other than that, yes, I'm sure. The whole hallway heard him say it."

"We were all shocked Dr. M would call anyone in the band a freak," Shweta said. "That's hate speech."

"What happened next?" Luce asked.

"Matt wheeled around and Dr. M slammed the door on him," Shweta said. "Matt banged on the door and then Dr. M opened it a bit—he'd put that bar thingy across the door—and he yelled for him to go away or he'd call security. Matt laughed and pointed at the guards right behind me and yelled, 'They're right here, mother effer!' Then Dr. M slammed the door again."

Luce looked at Banks. "I think we should have a word with our friend."

Matt the megabat seemed to be waiting for them. The door to his room was open, allowing a clear view across the room to the open balcony, where he stood at the railing, basking in the neon, wind ruffling his poncho. Luce called a hello and Matt waved them forward.

The sun had set over Sunset Strip and all the buildings were aglow. Across the street rose the faux Manhattan skyline of the New York–New York Casino, their mock Lady Liberty summoning the poor, the tired, and the gullible yearning to be free of their life savings.

"I know what you're going to ask me," Matt said. "What is it like to be a bat?" One ear pivoted like a radar dish, then the other. "Thomas Nagel? The mind-body problem? Anybody?"

"I was going to ask you if you could fly," Luce said.

"Ooh! You think I flew over to Dr. M's and killed him?"

Matt was slightly shorter than Tusk, but his narrow face and long neck made him seem taller. He wore a gold earring through one pert ear, which wasn't visible in the publicity pictures Luce had seen—too risqué for the tweeners? What was more surprising, when you got up close, was how furry he was. His head was covered by golden fuzz, and the back of his neck was a thick maroon ruff. His most famous features, his wings, were hidden beneath the poncho.

Luce said, "I saw you fly on a music video, but it looked a little fake."

"You're right. I wish I could fly, but physics has conspired against me. Have you ever heard of the square-cube law?"

"Humor me," she said.

"I'm trying, I'm trying! Tough crowd. Okay, if you square the area of an object, you cube the mass. I'm about twice the height and twice the wingspan of the largest bat, the golden-crowned flying fox—which means I've got, basically, four times the wing power. But that comes with eight times the mass—minimum. And I'm way heavier than a fruit bat. Those fuckers are three pounds! Which means, if I jump off this balcony, and I flap really really hard, I *still* hit the pavement at terminal velocity."

"Ouch."

"The only flying I do is on wires. For the live shows they rig me up and fling me out across the audience. It fucking kills me, but the kids love it."

"My daughter certainly does."

"A fan, huh? Does she know Mom's investigating her favorite band?"

Luce grinned. "I didn't say you were her favorite."

"I bet it's those fucking Backstreet Boys. Before we get into it, can I get you something to eat, or drink?"

"It's not larvae, is it?" Banks asked.

"Ha! You've been hanging out with little Timmy. I was thinking popcorn."

Track 11

"Left Hangin'"

Featuring Matt M. Bat

Matt led them inside and gestured for the detectives to sit at the kitchenette's bar. He put a popcorn bag into the microwave and set the timer. "Pellegrino? Pellegrino?"

"Sure," Detective Delgado said. She looked tired. He felt sorry she'd been dragged into this whole mess. Banks asked if he had any objections to being recorded, and Matt said it was fine.

"Any closer to catching the killer?" he asked them.

"We're working on it," Delgado said.

"I don't want to get into racial profiling here, but . . ." Matt popped open a can with one claw. "Statistically, your killer's got to be human. How many human-animal hybrids have committed murder? Zero. But the number of murders humans have perpetrated? It's off the charts! Murder's kind of your thing."

The timer went off and Matt gingerly picked up the edge of the steaming bag and set it on the counter. "Could you open that?" he asked Banks, and then reached up to a cabinet for a bowl.

"I shouldn't tell you this," Matt said, "but I'm a big mystery reader. The barge had a couple of Agatha Christies, and when I got out I tore through all the classics—Agatha Christie, Dorothy Sayers, John Dickson Carr."

"Why shouldn't you tell us that?" Banks asked. He shook the bag into the bowl.

"Because in those stories, guys who read mysteries are automatically suspicious."

"That happens a lot? Characters inside mysteries read mysteries?"

"All the time. Lord Peter Wimsey's always referencing Sherlock Holmes, Carr stops the plot so Dr. Fell can give a lecture on his favorite mystery writers. Poirot and Hastings have an entire conversation in *The ABC Murders* about how there's always a second murder in these stories, because it's more exciting—and Christie puts in three murders! I mean, they're all writing this stuff in the 1920s and they're already doing metafiction."

"I hate metafiction," Delgado said.

Banks said, "A couple hours ago she was telling me we're either in a locked-room mystery or a science fiction story. She said she really doesn't want to be in sci-fi."

"First, don't say 'sci-fi'—it's vulgar. But she's right, science fiction gives you no closure. At least in a mystery or thriller you return to the status quo, but in SF it's all epiphanies and trapdoors and space babies—space babies all the way down." Matt dipped a claw into the bowl. "Man, I love this fake butter."

"We were hoping you could answer a few questions," Delgado said. "Could you tell us when you left the party and where you were all night?"

"Right! Back to business. I have to tell you, I don't have

much of an alibi. I left the party when everybody else did, then went to my room. I came out this morning when I heard Bobby yelling."

"You didn't quite leave when everyone else did," Delgado said. "You were the last out, yes?"

"That's true."

"You want to tell us what you were arguing about with Dr. M?"

"Oh God, that. What weren't we arguing about? He was being such an asshole. Did Tusk tell you about the lawsuit?"

"He did," Banks said.

Matt shook his head. "My feeling is, there's enough money to go around. But Tusk and Tim feel like their work's been stolen, so I get that. And Maury, he wants *all* the money, the whole cash cow, down to the hooves. I was happy to walk away, but last night he told me if I went to school and missed a single performance he'd sue for breach of contract. So that pretty much pushed me to side with the boyz."

Delgado said, "What did Dr. M mean when he said— Banks, what was that again?"

Banks looked at his notebook and read aloud, "'You think I won't tell the fucking world about you freaks.'"

Delgado was studying Matt's face. It made him nervous. Did she see a monster, or a friendly neighborhood bat man?

"That pissed me off, but he's kind of right," Matt said. "We are freaks. Freaks of science. Who's our nearest competitor? Dolly the Sheep? I'll admit she's a looker, and seems to have a great personality, despite all the attention. Fame can change a person, you know?"

Delgado started to interrupt, but he kept rolling. "This is important—this is why I'm going to school in genetics, it's a much bigger mystery than who killed Maurice Bendix."

"What mystery is that?" Delgado asked.

"Dolly's just a clone. The WyldBoyZ, we're in a whole different game, genetic-engineering-wise. Think about all the steps needed to make a fully functioning member of this band—and I'd like some credit for passing up an easy joke about Devin and fully functioning members."

"Granted?" Banks said.

"Okay, imagine starting with the genome of one base human," Matt continued. "You fiddle with his genes, maybe give him a sequence that occurs in sheep. This is tricky. In genetics, you can't just change one thing—there's not just the single gene, but the expression of the gene, and the proteins manufactured by the gene. So many things can go wrong just by changing a base pair—think of Tay-Sachs disease, or sickle cell anemia, or cystic fibrosis, and those are the survivable mutations. Most fetuses with damaged genes don't make it to birth. But okay. Let's say that Mr. Sheep survives, and develops curly armpit hair that makes a fabulous sweater. Great! But he still doesn't look much like a sheep, and no one points to him and says, 'You should join an all-sheep band.' I don't know what that would be—Baaaad Company?"

"Ewe-2," Banks said.

"Ha! High five." Matt raised a wing and Banks slapped the palmish area where claws exited the fabric of skin.

"But we need to go further," Matt said. "Let's say, through years and years of brilliant yet thoroughly evil research in a thoroughly evil secret lab floating in international waters, you end up with a true miracle, a person who looks like a Photoshop blend of sheep and *Homo sapiens*, with a human-quality brain and the vocal apparatus for speech, which means vocal cords, mobile lips and tongue, a host of muscular and neuronal equipment to make it all work. And this man-sheep can not only talk, he can sing! Beautifully!"

"Really lays down the bleats," Banks said.

"Oh God, that's terrible," Matt said. "We've got to hang out."

"Says the bat."

"So that's the mystery of the lab?" Delgado said. She'd been writing something in her own notebook and put down her pencil. "How they achieved something so much more advanced than everybody else?"

"No, here's the real mystery—how do you do it again, with a completely different animal? Let's say a ferret. Fine. Decades later, you've achieved a second cross-species hybrid. Ta-da! Now, how do you do that *five times*?"

"Not just five," Delgado said. The firmness in her voice surprised him.

"What now?" Matt said.

"We already know there was a sixth subject—Tim calls her Sofia."

Matt picked up his Pellegrino, winced, and set it back down. "Well, fuck." He was dying to take another painkiller. He'd put off the next dose, wanting to stay sharp until he talked to the detectives. But now they wanted to delve into ancient history, and he would greatly appreciate a little chemical buffer.

He walked to the bed and sat. Suddenly he was conscious of his bare feet. They were built for hanging upside down, though Matt had never been able to sleep that way. Leftover anatomy.

"We don't talk about this," Matt said. "That's our rule. Not to the press, and hardly to each other."

"I'm not interested in selling your story to the tabloids," Delgado said. "Banks, turn off the recorder."

Banks looked surprised at this but did as he was told.

"Okay," Matt said. "There was another subject. The staff called her Subject One, but she told us to call her S. She was way older than us, and they put her through a lot. Painful procedures, forced isolation, forced pregnancies. I think they even—"

"What the hell?" Delgado said. "*Pregnancies?*"

I've said too much, Matt thought. Delgado was shocked, and her eyes were shining. This was one of the reasons the boyz had agreed to never talk about the horrors of the barge. They did not want to be seen as victims, as helpless lab rats. But now he was forced to explain.

"They were chemically induced," Matt said. "Subject One had a talent for parthenogenesis, no sperm required, and they were interested in that."

"Who's 'they'?" Delgado said. She was angry and trying to keep a lid on it.

"Americans, obviously. Why do you think we talk this way? The staff were all American, and all the books and videotapes and CDs in the library were American, too. In English anyway. We didn't think we were American, but we didn't think we weren't, either. Does that make sense? It's all we knew, so of course we wanted to come here when Dr. M made the offer."

Banks asked, "Were they US military? Government scientists?"

"We can't prove anything. They didn't have uniforms, they flew no flags, and nobody said the Pledge of Allegiance. The barge was no Navy ship—it was old, and all the high-tech parts came in as shipping containers: whole labs, bolted together on the deck. Still, we're all pretty convinced they were government backed. It was the Cold War, and as Tim says, who else has got the resources to do what they did? But we don't talk about that in the press. We just say 'evil scientists' and let it go at that."

"But the CIA hasn't come for you," Banks said. "Nobody's grabbed you since your rescue."

"Or have they?" Delgado asked.

"No," Matt said. "Nobody's whisked us off to a black site. The only scientific experiments we've been part of, we volunteered for. I pushed the guys into doing some of them, for medical reasons. That may have backfired, though—I made Tim so paranoid about our lack of knowledge about ourselves that he got a little obsessed with it."

"Why do you think no government's tried to grab you?" she asked. "You're unique. Every sci-fi—sorry, every science fiction movie says they would have put you in quarantine."

Because we're famous, Matt thought. That, and their money, was their only protection.

Matt shrugged. "Maybe they learned everything they could from us. They got their data, and they moved on."

"What about Sofia?" Delgado said. "What happened to her?"

"We left her."

Delgado waited for him to say more. He decided to tell them the truth.

"There was an explosion somewhere deep in the ship. It was the middle of the night and fires were breaking out. The guards wouldn't let us out of our cells, even when the smoke started rolling through. They all took off to somewhere else on the ship, leaving us there. Finally, someone took pity on us, and unlocked the doors. We ran to a lifeboat, hit the winch, and dropped into the water. Turns out we didn't pick the best boat—the motor wouldn't work. Some guards saw us, started firing at us from the deck. Tusk rolled over the side and fucking *towed* us through the water to get away."

He glanced up, and Delgado's eyes were fixed on him. Banks scribbled in his notebook.

"You want to know why Tim feels so guilty?" Matt said. "We *are* guilty. We didn't even *try* to help Sofia. We left her alone on the barge and ran."

"You were kids," Delgado said.

"Sure. We were kids, and we were panicked and scared, all of that. But we knew what we were doing. We were leaving her to die."

Track 12

"Home [extended version]"

Featuring Detective Delgado

Matt had finally run out of words. Luce thought it was risky to keep pushing and have him clam up altogether, but she was running out of time, and she needed answers.

"Did Dr. M know about Sofia?" she asked.

"Bobby told him," Matt answered. "Bobby always trusted Maury, and Maury took advantage. But there's no proof. Everything went down with the ship. But we don't talk about her, because . . . well, we're a fucking boy band. We're not The Cure."

Banks' cell phone rang. He answered and said, "Oh, good. Thanks for the update." To Luce he said, "That was the officer who drove Mrs. M. They're back."

Matt got to his feet. "Are we done?"

Luce walked to him and shook his hand. "I appreciate you sharing all that."

Banks said, "I hope we get to hang out, buddy," and clapped him on the shoulder. Matt squeaked in pain.

"Whoa!" Banks said. "You okay?"

"I'm fine. That flying contraption I told you about? I

torqued my shoulder last night. Last show of the tour and that's my souvenir."

"Oh, sorry about that."

"I'm just glad I don't have to get in that thing again."

"If we don't see you before the morning," Luce said, "have a safe flight."

———————

They walked down to the elevator. The door to the penthouse suite was closed now and sealed with yellow crime scene tape. Luce touched the button for 56, one floor down.

"So what was that about?" Banks asked.

When they were sitting at Matt's kitchenette bar, Luce had written in her notebook: WHEN WE GO GRAB HIM BY THE RIGHT SHOULDER. She'd left the page open until Banks had seen it.

"He wasn't using his right arm," Luce said. "That whole time with the drinks and the popcorn, everything was his left hand. When I shook his hand I could tell he was in pain. And when you hit the shoulder, he couldn't hide it."

"You don't believe him about the flying contraption?"

"I don't, but we're going to have to talk to crew people to know for sure, see if they reported any malfunction, or if he complained at the time."

"If he's lying, how do you think he— Wait. The balcony door. The crack in it. You think he flew into it?"

"He's not lying about the physics. I'm sure he can't fly."

"So . . . what? He had a fight with Dr. M? They were alone for a couple minutes. Not enough time to kill him, and the two zoomies said that Dr. M—"

"Zoomandos."

"Sorry, I meant to say Trekkies. Dr. M locked the door, then yelled at Matt."

"Bendix was alive and behind a locked door at three AM, no doubt about that," Luce said. The elevator opened and they stepped out. "Which number is hers?"

"Fifty-Six Sixteen," he said. On this floor the rooms were smaller and there were more of them. "She's the last interview, right?"

"I need to do this one alone," Luce said.

"You sure?"

"I think it'll go better, woman to woman. Could you do me a favor? Call the coroner's office, find out who's doing the autopsy, and tell them that I absolutely need the results of the blood work, tonight."

"What's going on? Was Dr. M poisoned? Did he OD?"

"I just want to confirm something."

"You know who did it!"

She did. What she didn't understand was *why* Dr. M was murdered. All the motives on the table didn't convince her. She said, "I don't want to get ahead of myself."

"Don't do this to me, I can see it in your face," Banks said. "Who is it? Not the fan—we haven't learned anything new. And not Matt. Did Tim go ballistic? Comes back, blood on his claws, washes up in the bathroom . . ."

"Tim barely scratched him. I think people at the party would have noticed if he clawed him apart."

"So he goes in after the zoomando leaves."

"While Bobby is next to the Doc in bed?"

"I got it," Banks said. "Tim's at the party and has poison on his claws, and then—never mind, that doesn't explain the clawing."

"I promise you, if I get proof of what happened, I'll let you know. Just try to get me those blood test results, okay? Beg and plead for me."

"I'll try."

"Thanks, Mickey."

He tilted his head. "You never call me by my first name."

"I won't let it happen again."

"I like it . . . Lucia."

"Aaagh! Go. That was a huge mistake."

"Okay, just call me if there's a second murder."

She watched him lope away. She wondered what kind of animal he'd make. Looked like an owl, walked like a wolf, but left the overall impression of a smart-alec giraffe. And what kind of animal was Luce Delgado? She didn't want to think about it.

She shook a breath, held it, then let it out. Here we go, she thought, and knocked.

———————

Marilyn Bendix stood by the bed, angrily going through a pile of skirts, tops, and shoes. She'd pick up a piece, scowl, and then throw it into one of the three open suitcases on the floor. A smaller carry-on bag was already zipped up. "Where the hell is my Versace bandeau? Canary yellow, rhinestones, matches the track pants."

"We couldn't give you all of your clothes," Luce said. "Some of them had blood on them, making them evidence."

"Blood? How did blood get on my clothes?"

Because the killer was looking for something, Luce thought. Aloud she said, "We're trying to figure that out. But after this is over, I promise you, if there's anything of value, we'll get it back for you."

"I don't want it back if it's got my husband's blood on it!"

"Understandable."

"Did you find the person who did this yet?"

"I'm sorry, no."

"They ripped him apart. Oh, the morgue people kept most of his body covered, but I could tell. I could *tell.*" She scooped a handful of glittery material and shoes and dropped them into one of the suitcases. "And now they say they can't release the body. I have to wait here, in this goddamn tourist trap, for who knows how long."

Even furious, Mrs. M looked put together. Luce had grown up with women like her: showgirls and burlesque performers who understood the transformational power of vivid makeup and structurally sound underwear. Luce's father had been clueless about "woman things," but these battle-hardened showbiz ladies had taken young Luce under their wing and taught her the essentials. When the girl went onstage, she looked like she belonged there. Luce had stopped putting in the effort when she left the magic act, but Marilyn Bendix was still onstage, engaged in a permanent performance as Mrs. M.

"I know this has to be hard," Luce said. "And complicated."

"Complicated? What the hell does that mean?"

"I've gone through a divorce. I know about mixed feelings."

"Who says I was going through a divorce?"

Luce sat down. It was usually a good de-escalation move. "I know when you left that room last night, you weren't planning on coming back."

"Did Devin say that? Devin's a kid." She must have realized how that sounded and quickly added, "A young man. Ape.

Whatever. He was a good lay, but he doesn't have anything to do with me."

"You walked out in a towel, Mrs. Bendix. But when I saw you this morning, you were wearing your clothes."

Mrs. M blinked. "So?"

"So, you either snuck back to the room, sometime after four thirty in the morning, got Dr. M to open the door for you, which makes you the last person to see your husband alive, or—"

"That never happened!"

"Or you packed a bag, before the party. You put it in Devin's room, because you knew you'd sleep there last night."

"So what? I wanted one last fuck."

Luce appreciated how quickly the woman changed tack. "And you stayed in Devin's room all night, until I saw you?"

"Yes. What are you getting at?"

"Devin didn't leave the room, either?"

"No."

"You're absolutely sure? Perhaps you dozed off and he slipped away."

"Sure, it's *possible*. But the way he sleeps—he wraps his arms and legs around you and holds on for dear life. At first it's kind of sweet, and then you think, oh my God, I'm going to suffocate. I barely slept."

"So, you're vouching for him."

Her eyes narrowed—and her intense black eyeliner added to the gun-barrel effect. "You think I'm covering for him, so Devin could kill my husband?"

"Or he's covering for you."

"*What?*"

Devin was right about her arms—the woman was toned.

Luce didn't doubt she could pull herself up the side of a building if she wanted to. A lot of cops underestimated the power of a determined woman.

Luce said, "I wanted to kill my ex, plenty of times. Especially when I realized he was lying to me about money."

"I didn't need to kill him to get what's mine."

"But that's the hard part, isn't it? Finding out what's yours. When I went through my breakup, it was a mess. See, I knew how much money *I* made, but my husband was a professional poker player. I could never get a straight answer from him on how much he'd put away in bank accounts, how much cash he had—and how big a debt he owed. I might have walked away, but I had a kid to take care of, so I went digging through the family computer."

Mrs. M had stopped looking through the suitcases—her attention was fully on Luce now.

"The computer belonged to both of us, but he'd encrypted a bunch of the files with a password. I couldn't see any of his banking information."

"What did you do?" Mrs. M asked.

"Luckily, we have this department, they do computer forensics. Real nerd stuff, with all the hacking software." This was a fib. The forensics guys were pretty good, but they were overworked and every job they performed left a paper trail. Luce had gone to her cousin for help. "Long story short," Luce said, "I have people who can open anything."

Mrs. M sat on the bed. "Anything?"

"Your husband had something on the WyldBoyZ, and I think it's on his laptop."

"Maury never discussed that with me. He never discussed anything. If there's dirt about the boyz, I don't know it."

"I believe you. He sounds like he was paranoid about that kind of thing. I think the killer was searching your room for that laptop, and couldn't find it. But if you could help me put my hands on it, that would go a long way toward proving you have nothing to hide, and had no part of the murder. My guys would crack the password, we'd make copies of the files we're interested in, and then give the laptop back to you. It's your property, after all."

"And the password?"

"We'd of course tell you what it is. Or just disable it and leave the laptop unlocked. Your choice."

Mrs. M stared at her. Then she stood and walked to the carry-on bag. Unzipped the top. Pulled out a black laptop.

"Unlocked," she said.

Luce had almost made it out of the hotel when Captain De-Andrea spotted her. She'd turned down the same hallway where they'd found the chipmunk suit and there he was, standing in front of the notorious restroom, expounding to two white men in suits and an uncomfortable Detective Banks. The captain called to her before she could wheel about and run.

"Detective! We were just talking about you. Let me introduce you to Agent Hammergarten and Agent Wilhelm."

Luce reluctantly shook hands with them. "Pleased to meet you!" one said. "We're fans of your work!" They were both as fit and aggro-cheery as spin class instructors.

"You're FBI?" The laptop she held at her side seemed to weigh a hundred pounds.

"Oh no, they'll be here in the morning, I'm sure," one of them said. She'd already forgotten which was which. "We're FWS."

"I've never heard of you."

"United States Fish and Wildlife Service," the other one said. "Anything regarding the WyldBoyZ falls under our purview."

"Oh, *purview*," she said. "Well, none of them are suspects at the moment, not even Bobby O. The captain told you about our current theory?"

"The FBI will handle the investigation—we're here on a related matter. Have you seen this man?"

He opened a file folder and handed it to her. Sitting on top was a black-and-white portrait, shot in harsh light, of a man with gray eyes, stiff black hair, and a face-swallowing black beard. Scars ran along his forehead. His expression, facing that camera, was defiant.

"Who is he?" she asked.

"Jorge Heriberto. A smuggler of endangered species—we've been tracking him for a while. Have you seen him? He might have shaved, obvs!"

"Captain," she said. "Have you heard of this guy?"

The captain said no but assured the agents he'd look into it.

"I haven't heard of him, either," Luce said. She closed the folder and handed it back to the agent. Her heart was beating fast, but she'd been performing under pressure since she was eight years old. "Then again, there's a lot of people running around in costumes, so who knows." She walked away, toward the fire exit.

The captain made captain noises and Luce said over her shoulder, "Have to pick up Melanie!"

The door sounded an alarm. She ignored it. The courtyard was brightly lit, and the warmth was a relief after the refrigerated atmosphere of the hotel.

The alarm blared again and Banks caught up to her. "Where are you going? The captain wants to do a press conference."

"Home." She kept walking toward the VIP lot.

"Are you okay?" Banks said. "You look like you saw a ghost."

Shit. Banks was getting to know her a little too well. She stopped and opened the laptop. Tucked between screen and keyboard was the photograph of Jorge Heriberto. "Did the fish police show you this?"

"Wait—how did you . . . ?"

"Just look at it. Does it remind you of anybody?"

He studied it closely, then his eyes widened. "Kat Vainikolo? Holy cow, you're right! No tattoos, but he could be her twin brother. What does *that* mean?"

"I don't know yet. Any word on the blood tests?"

"They're still working on them. But get this: Lionel found a hair—inside the chipmunk suit."

"Hair, or fur?"

"Turns out, they're chemically indistinguishable—we just call it hair when humans have it. But this one's thick and black, like, *Devin-quality* hair."

Luce didn't speak for a moment, and Banks said, "I thought you would have been more excited about this. This could put Devin in the suit! Which means Mrs. M was covering for him. Devin climbs up the building, goes down the other side, and walks out in the suit."

Luce took a breath. "Okay, that's all good stuff. I need to chew on it."

"You want to tell me where you found the laptop?"

"Mrs. M had it. Call me as soon as you've got something from the blood test."

She started walking and Banks said, "What about the press conference?"

"You do it. Just look into the camera and be boring. Don't smile. And for Christ sake, no jokes."

She walked to her car and put the laptop on the floor on the passenger side. Called a number on her cell and was relieved when he picked up. "Manuel, it's Luce. How you doing?"

"How *you* doing, Cousin? Solve any murders today?"

"Getting close. I need a favor—I'm having a tech support emergency. Can you come by tonight? I'll make you dinner."

"Oh hell no."

"I mean I'll *buy* you dinner. How about Serrano's?"

"That's more like it. Can't wait to see Melanie—I haven't seen her since her birthday! So what's the nature of your IT emergency?"

"I'll have to tell you when you get there. Bring all your tools."

Melanie sat in the passenger seat, holding the takeout bag, practically vibrating with excitement. "So who was the nicest? Was it Tusk? I bet it was Tusk. Do you know he named himself after a Fleetwood Mac song?"

"Tusk was very polite. They were all nice. Please don't put your feet on the laptop."

"Did you meet Tim? He's the shy one, sometimes he gets so shy he can't even *talk*."

Luce was heartsick. How was she going to tell Melanie that

the band would never sing together again and it was her mother's fault? She might as well have lined them up and shot them all down on Sunset Strip. The Moreau Massacre.

"Mami, no one's going to believe me. If I call Chloe can you tell her that you met them?"

"Sweetie, no. You can't tell anyone about this, not right now. It's an open case. You're sworn to police secrecy, okay?"

Manuel's Audi Twin Turbo roared in three minutes after Luce pulled in the driveway. The power of the Serrano's green shrimp enchiladas was strong.

Her cousin was only twenty-nine, but he was already in demand as an electronic security consultant. Casinos had gotten very nervous about people sneaking computers into the gaming rooms or communicating wirelessly with confederates. Manuel, the teenage phone phreak, had gone legit. Well, mostly legit. He still did favors for his older cousin, such as breaking into an ex-husband's encrypted files.

After they finished with the enchiladas (for the adults) and flautas (for the nine-year-old), Manuel said, "So what do you got?"

Luce opened the ThinkPad. "It's password protected and I need to get into it. It looks like it's running Windows 98. Is that hard to break into?"

Manuel frowned. "Windows 98? Wow. Okay, let me think. I'm going to need a fork."

"A fork?"

"Please."

Luce went to the kitchen and came back. "Okay, now what do you—hey!"

The screen was open and showing File Explorer. Manuel took a USB drive out of the side and put it in his pocket.

"How did you do that?" she asked.

Melanie fell out laughing. Manuel said to the girl, "When I was younger than you, your mom did this amazing card trick—the card I picked *jumped* into her mouth. I begged and begged her to tell me how she did it, and do you know what she said? 'If I tell you, it wouldn't be magic, it would just be a dumb trick.'"

"You got burned, Mami! Burned!"

"So what's the fork for?" Luce said.

Manuel opened his arms. "Flan!"

After dessert, Luce asked him how to find a CD image file on the hard disk. "I think the guy who owned this laptop conned some people. They gave him a CD to play, and he copied the whole thing while they thought he was just playing it. Then later, he burned it again to CD. Is that possible?"

"Sure, let me look. Okay, here's a bunch of ISO images, let me find the CUE file—okay, yes."

"Yes? Do you see MP3 files? I'm looking for music."

"No MP3s, but there are a bunch of WAV files. The first ten tracks of the CD are audio—those will play fine in a CD player—then there's a bunch of data files stacked on to the last track. Images, mostly."

"If you transfer those to CD, can I see the images on another PC?"

"Not a problem."

"Okay, burn it again, the whole CD."

In six minutes she was holding a CD that she hoped was the copy of the one Dr. M had put in the CD player.

"Manuel, you're the best."

"Say my name."

Melanie shouted, "Manuel!"

"Say my hacker name!"

"Manuel Override!"

Manuel swept up Melanie in his arms, spun her around. "You bet, princesa!"

——————

An hour later, Luce was on the couch, her legs resting on her dad's old *Trunk of Mystery!*, which they used as a coffee table. Melanie sat curled up next to her. Luce turned down the TV and put the CD into her laptop. Windows Media Player popped up, and she clicked Play.

Tusk was right: The recording was rough. There was a long section of dead air, with some low rumble in the background. Voices were talking far away from the microphone. Then, suddenly, a voice sang one long, pure note.

Melanie matched it.

"What is that?" Luce asked her.

"Concert pitch, Mami." She rolled her eyes. "A over middle C."

Voices joined, one by one, each on a different note until it became one massive chord. It sounded like a church organ. Melanie laughed in delight. "It's them! Can you hear them? That's Tusk on the low note and Matt's way way up there—"

"You can tell that it's them?" Luce asked.

"Duh." The notes began to move around as if they were pulling on each other. Melanie said, "That's 'Home'! Listen!"

Luce had heard the song, but she couldn't pull out the melody from this wall of harmony. And then Melanie began to sing:

"There's a place for us floating on the sea,
Where the wind is sweet and we are free. . . ."

It was undeniably the WyldBoyZ song. "Okay, how about this one?" Luce asked, and clicked on track 2.

"Easy, that's 'One of a Kind,'" Melanie said. "Hear it?" She sang:

"I used to be just a boy in a band,
Knew I'd been dealt a losing hand,
No chance to win, and what do I get,
One last card and one last bet."

Luce knew the chorus and joined in:

"Then you walked in,
You walked in and you were . . .
One of a kiiiiind. . . ."

They played every track on the copied CD. Melanie could identify them all. Luce preferred these a capella, wordless versions of the songs to the ones on the WyldBoyZ albums, but it might have been because she loved to hear Melanie singing along. Where had this talent come from? Not from Luce, and certainly not from her father. It was a genetic mystery.

"This is so weird," Melanie said. "That woman—the one who sang the first note, who keeps singing a lot of the melody—did they *add* her to the band?" This was clearly sacrilege.

"No, mija," Luce said. "I think it's the other way around. She was there first."

Melanie didn't understand, and then Luce said, "I think that's Sofia."

Melanie's squeal could have come straight from Matt the bat. "I knew it!" she said. "I knew she was real."

Melanie asked her to replay the wordless version of "Deep Down," the one about Sofia, but the television caught Luce's eye. She reached to turn up the volume and Melanie said, "It's Bobby O!"

The news anchor was talking over footage of Bobby walking out of the municipal building. Luce turned up the volume. The cat man stopped at the front steps and waved to the cameras. "I'm free!" he shouted. "I'm free, everybody!"

Then they cut to tape of Captain DeAndrea's press conference, which had happened hours ago. The captain described how LVMPD was working the case but did not yet have a named suspect. Reporters asked if they could describe the suspect, and the captain nodded to Detective Banks, who swallowed hard and stepped up to the microphone. "All we can say for the moment is this," Banks said—and here he looked directly at the KTNV Action News camera. "We think it was a rabid fan."

Luce shouted, "God damn it, Banks!"

"Mami!" Melanie said. "Language."

———

Luce decided to do the rest of the work in bed and let Melanie climb in with her. The girl fell asleep against her, pinning Luce's left arm and turning the skin there into a sweaty patch. It was uncomfortable and made it awkward to work the laptop, but Luce wasn't about to move her. How many more years of cuddling would she get from the girl?

There were more than a hundred image files on the disc, all with autogenerated file names like *scn-05058002.tif*. She'd already clicked through them, looking for photos, and was a bit disappointed that the images were all photocopies of documents: handwritten memos and typed scientific reports she couldn't make heads or tails out of, with titles like "Anomalous Transcription Factors in Key Melanocytic Genes." Most of the reports were dated in the 1970s and '80s, but a few went back to the '50s. Sometime near midnight she opened one with the title "Subject Index." The first two paragraphs were instructions for updating this form, but then there was this:

- SUBJECT 1. DOB (EST): 1837. CUSTODY: JUNE 5, 1953. MASTER FILE: M01-001-1.

Luce read the line again. "What the fuck?" Date of birth 1837? There was nothing else about Subject 1. But the list continued:

- SUBJECT 2. DOB: MAY 2, 1955. FEMALE. TERMINATED: MAY 15, 1955. URSINE FEATURES. MASTER FILE: M02-278.
- SUBJECT 3. DOB: APRIL 17, 1956. MALE. TERMINATED: DECEMBER 21, 1962. BOVINE FEATURES. MASTER FILE: M03-344.
- SUBJECT 4. DOB: MARCH 25, 1957. FEMALE. TERMINATED: APRIL 17, 1957. CANINE FEATURES. MASTER FILE: M04-381.
- SUBJECT 5. DOB: FEBRUARY 11, 1958. FEMALE. TERMINATED: MARCH 11, 1958. XENARTHRAN FEATURES. MASTER FILE: M05-388.

- SUBJECT 6. DOB: NOVEMBER 14, 1958. UNDIFFERENTI-
ATED. TERMINATED: NOVEMBER 14, 1958. MASTER FILE:
M05-388.

It went on and on, a new birth every seven or eight months. Every female was terminated within weeks of being born. Every male was killed before the age of thirteen. The "undifferentiated" were terminated immediately.

Only at the end of the file did she finally find a child who was still alive:

- SUBJECT 27: DOB: JULY 28, 1977. MALE. ELEPHANTIDAEN
FEATURES. MASTER FILE M27-923 (ONGOING).
- SUBJECT 28: DOB: JULY 7, 1978. MALE. CHIROPTERAN FEA-
TURES. MASTER FILE M28-1001 (ONGOING).
- SUBJECT 29: DOB: MARCH 25, 1979. UNDIFFERENTIATED.
TERMINATED: MARCH 25, 1979. MASTER FILE M29-1011.
- SUBJECT 30: DOB: FEBRUARY 13, 1980. FEMALE. TERMI-
NATED: MARCH 17, 1980. FELINE FEATURES. MASTER FILE
M30-1020.
- SUBJECT 31: DOB: DECEMBER 23, 1980. MALE. PRIMATE
FEATURES. MASTER FILE: M31-1032 (ONGOING).
- SUBJECT 32: DOB: DECEMBER 12, 1981. MALE. PHOLI-
DOTAN FEATURES. SEE FILE M32-1078 (ONGOING).
- SUBJECT 33: DOB: JUNE 2, 1983. MALE. FELINE FEATURES.
SEE FILE M34-1111 (ONGOING).

Her cell phone went off, vibrating the bedside table. Luce came back to herself, realized her eyes were swimming with tears. She picked up the phone. It was Banks. She could barely speak.

"Oh, Delgado, did I wake you up? Sorry to call after midnight, but you said you wanted to know."

"I'm up." She cleared her throat. "What is it?"

"A bunch of things. First, the blood on the costume and claws matches Dr. M's blood type. We'll be able to do a DNA match soon, but it looks good. Plus, the pharmaceutical screens came back. They found quite a few illicit substances in Dr. M's bloodstream, but there was a lot of something called Anectine—which is, um, let me read it: succinylcholine chloride. It's a serious muscle relaxant—so serious it can give you a heart attack."

"Is it a party drug?"

"Strictly medical. But it comes as a white powder. So guess what that plate in Dr. M's bedroom tested positive for?"

"Right. That makes sense." Luce heard a noise outside—it sounded like a car door closing. She eased away from Melanie until the girl's head dropped onto the pillow. The girl barely stirred.

"You okay?" Banks asked. "You sound a little . . . I don't know."

"I found the second murder," Luce said. "And the next one, and another dozen."

"*What?* Where?"

Luce went to the window and looked through the blinds. She had a view to the street but didn't see anything.

"I'll explain later," Luce said. "Listen, the feds are taking over in the morning. The band's leaving at nine. Meet me at the hotel at, say, seven."

"Are we, uh, arresting someone?"

"Oh yeah."

———

Detective Mickey Banks, God bless him, was waiting for her with coffee. "You look like you could use it," he said.

"I stayed up late, and woke up early. Couldn't sleep." She thought she was tired yesterday, but now her body felt like it had been lightly pummeled by preteen boxers. "Ready?"

"It would really help if you told me who we were arresting."

"I haven't decided yet." She felt terrible lying to him. But she needed to get through this part of the performance. He needed to stay in the dark, at least until he'd finished talking to the feds. Banks had a long, fruitful career ahead of him, and she didn't want to derail it.

They walked into the lobby. They'd just reached the rotunda of elevators when Rudolfo ran up to them. His cologne caught up a second later. "Detective Delgado! Detective Banks! Such a morning. The other officers are already upstairs. If there's anything I can do, please let me—"

"Other officers?" Luce said.

He blinked. "Two men in suits. They weren't happy when I told them about the checkouts, but they insisted on going up anyway."

"Slow down," Banks said. "Who checked out?"

The elevator door opened. Inside were the FWS agents, Hammergarten and Wilhelm. One of them pointed at Luce. "You! What the fuck did you do?" Both the men were furious—cheeriness gone, pure aggro now.

Banks, bless him, tried to step in front of Luce, but the agent—Hammergarten?—shoved him out of the way.

Luce looked up at him. "You'd better back the fuck up, Agent."

Hammergarten's neck bulged above his white collar in a festive shade of red. "That fucking trick with the photograph. You recognized him. You tipped him off."

"As I tried to say," Rudolfo put in. "The band checked out of their rooms last night, all of them, except for Mrs. Bendix."

"Those animals are government property," Agent Wilhelm said.

"If you let them escape," Hammergarten spat into Luce's face, "we will *bury* you."

"Should've listened," Luce said. A loud click. Hammergarten looked down and found that his wrist had been handcuffed to his belt.

"What the fuck? How did you—?" He yanked on the cuffs, and she pushed him away from her.

"I didn't 'tip them off,'" she said. "I came here to arrest one of them for murder."

"Ooh! Which one?" Rudolfo asked.

"She won't say," Banks said.

"Good luck finding them," Luce said. She strode away from them, toward the front door. Banks hurried to catch up.

"I'll call the airport," Banks said. "We can stop them."

"They were going on a private jet," Luce said. "If they went to the airport last night, they're long gone."

"Then I'll call the local cops. They were flying to Orlando? Maybe it hasn't landed yet. I can get someone to—"

"They weren't going to Orlando," Luce said. "They never were. They had somewhere else in mind—somewhere pretty far away."

"Yeah? Where's that?"

———

Six hours earlier, Luce had heard a second car door slam. She opened the drawer of the bedside table and took her Glock 22 from the holster. Thumb checked the safety.

Easy does it, she told herself. Think calming thoughts.

She walked to the front of the house. Looked through the peephole. An elephant man was walking up the front door. Behind him were more shapes, each one distinct.

Luce opened the door—not all the way. She kept the gun out of sight.

Tusk stopped. Lifted a big hand. He wore a green tailored jacket, a green vest, and a red bow tie. "Hello, Detective." Kat stepped up beside him. Behind them were Matt, Devin, Bobby, and tiny Tim.

"Detective Delgado!" Bobby said. "They let me out!"

"I see that," Luce said.

"We apologize for intruding at this late hour," Tusk said. "We'd hoped to talk to you in the morning, but Bobby's release, and the arrival of certain parties at the hotel, made us reevaluate the departure time, and so we thought we'd stop by on our way out of town."

"And how the fuck did you know where I lived?" Luce asked.

Matt ruffled his poncho. "I am . . . Batman."

"I know why you're here," Luce said. "It's not going to happen."

They wanted the laptop. The whole murder had been about the contents on its hard drive.

"We just want to talk," Kat said.

"With peace in our hearts," Devin said.

"And answer any of your questions," Tusk added.

Luce did have a lot of questions. She let them see the gun but kept it at her side. "My daughter's in the other room."

"We promise to be quiet," Tusk said.

The room filled with WyldBoyZ. Tusk eased himself onto the couch, taking up most of it, and Tim climbed up beside him. Devin had paused to look at a show poster, showing a teenage Luce and her father, in matching tuxes. Bobby gawked at the sword cabinet.

Kat took one of the remaining chairs. Dr. M's laptop sat atop the *Trunk of Mystery!*, within her reach. Luce picked up the laptop, opened the trunk, and put it inside.

Kat raised an eyebrow, and an entire row of tattoos shifted with it.

"Where do you want to start?" Tusk asked.

"Do the reveal!" Matt said. "That's the best part. I was so afraid we were going to miss it."

"You want *me* to explain?" Luce said.

"We guessed that you've figured everything out," Tusk said. "Are we wrong?"

"I actually have two explanations." Luce took the seat closest to the hallway to the bedrooms. "I have a simple solution, monsieur, and a complicated one."

Matt laughed, as she knew he would. "Classic," he said.

"Why don't you start with the simple one," Kat said.

"It's not me, is it?" Bobby asked.

"It's not you," Luce said. "If there's anyone who's innocent, it's you."

"Oh good!" He dropped to the floor beside Kat's chair. Kat put her hand on his head and scritched. "I want to hear this."

"Let's call the simple solution the Rabid Fan theory," Luce said. "A young and attractive sociopath, furious with Dr. M, came to the party last night with a plan for murdering him."

"How do you know they were young and attractive?" Devin asked.

"I'll get to it. They're most probably a fan of yours, and not a—what did you call them, Kat? A backstreet bitch. No, it's more likely they're a true zoomando, maybe even an LTZ."

"You've certainly picked up on the fucking lingo," Kat said.

"Word got out that the band was breaking up," Luce continued. "So this young, mentally unstable fan, totally dedicated to the WyldBoyZ, decides Dr. M is to blame."

"The Yoko," Devin intoned.

"Oh no," Matt added.

"Why do you think it might be a Long Term Zoomando?" Tusk asked. "It could be anybody who loved us."

"Because they had to know a lot of inside information to pull off this murder," Luce said. "They had to know about the party, and they had to know they could pass muster with Shweta and Gordon. Most important, they had to know that Dr. M regularly took young fans to bed."

"To be fair," Devin said, "that's a pretty good guess with any music producer."

"Sure. But the plan doesn't work if they can't flirt with the doctor and get into that bedroom, on that night, guaranteed."

"Ooh, which is why they'd have to be young and attractive," Devin said.

"And a sociopath," Tusk said, "because they didn't just kill Dr. M, they tore him apart."

"And how do you know the condition of the body?" Luce asked.

"Mrs. M told Devin about it. But why are you so sure it was premeditated? It could be an impulsive act."

"Not a chance," Luce said. "Those claws were custom-built

for murder—definitely not decorative."

"And not on-brand, chipmunk-wise," Matt said.

"That costume was store-bought, and disposable. That threw me off for a bit—why handcraft the claws but not make a custom suit? Then I met your fan club president. Any well-made costume would be as recognizable as a signature, at least to other fans. So, the killer had to keep the costume hidden until they needed it. Maybe they kept it in a bag, or hid it in Dr. M's bedroom at the start of the party. Then, after the murder, they went downstairs, dumped the costume, and walked out—without their face being seen."

"Never to be found?" Tusk asked.

"Between the names you gave us, and Shweta and Gordon's list, we were able to identify most of the guests. It's just a matter of policework to track down each person and confirm where they were between three and five AM. From there we'll just start eliminating suspects."

"Wow!" Bobby said. "That's so cool. I was *pretty* sure it wasn't me? But it's good to hear."

Luce said, "Bobby, you showed up in the doctor's suite after the killer left, and then immediately snorted up a lot of medical-grade muscle relaxant. You were out cold."

"It wasn't cocaine?"

"Sorry, no. Somehow, Dr. M's dealer slipped him a drug called Anectine. It's also a white powder."

"That's weird," Bobby said.

"In the simple solution, the Rabid Fan theory, the alternate drug's just a red herring," Luce said. "It has nothing to do with the murder."

"In the simple solution," Tusk said.

"So," Kat said. "Maybe we should hear the complicated one?"

"You want me to do this in front of Bobby?" Luce asked.

"Why can't you do it in front of me?"

"He should hear it," Tim said. "He's not a child anymore." It was the first time the pangolin had spoken since he'd entered the room. "Tell it, Detective."

Track 13

"Killer Track"

The WyldBoyZ

Dear Detective Delgado—Excuse me for intruding on the story. Rather than repeating what you told us that night, I thought you might prefer the following, completely true account, fleshed out with telling detail.

Matt stood on the edge of the roof, his toe claws gripping the edge. "Come on, man, you can do this," he said to himself. He pulled on one elbow, then the other, limbering up. Stretched out his wings. "A one, and a two, and a—"

He froze. Then, slowly, he leaned over the edge again and looked down along the Matador's brightly lit walls. They were virulent green, or so he was told. Dr. M's balcony—the wider one, which led to the lounge—lay thirty feet below him and slightly to the left. The stiff updraft pushed at his wings in a taunting way. He remembered a joke about hotels and updrafts that ended with the punch line "You're a real dick, Superman." Not a good thought. Concentrate, Matt!

He checked the harness again. It was the same contraption he used onstage, but instead of multiple cables connecting him to the rig above the stage, there was a single bungee cord tied around a flagpole. Oh! And no stunt coordinator to watch over him.

He was naked except for his boxer shorts and the harness, on the theory that lighter = better, but now he wished he'd brought more equipment: a helmet, for example. When he'd practiced bungee jumping at a tourist trap, he'd worn lots of protective gear.

He checked his watch. Three fifty-seven. Shit! Time to fly.

He jumped before he could talk himself out of it. The wind caught him—and immediately sent him sluicing sideways. He stifled a scream and stiffened his arms. The wind jerked him nearly upright—stall position—and then he began to plummet. This time he did scream.

Some bat instinct kicked in and he curled up, which brought his face down. He threw out his wings again and womp! a solid cushion of air buoyed him up.

Ha! He was flying! Well, gliding.

But now he was zooming away from the hotel. Suddenly the bungee cord went taut—and jerked him backwards. He was going to slam into the wall! He twisted in a frenzy and managed to turn his body around. His vision filled with the expanse of glowing glass. He fixed his eyes on the balcony. All he had to do was coast up, clear the railing, and then quickly fold his wings and drop onto the cement.

The wall raced toward him. Too fast! Too fast! He flashed his wings, caught air—and slammed into the sliding glass door, shoulder first.

The pain was *amazing*.

He lay on the balcony, moaning. He was sure he'd blown it; the sound of the crash would have woken the dead and maybe even the (hopefully unconscious) Dr. M.

He couldn't move his right arm and was convinced he'd shattered a bone. He managed to unclip from the bungee cord with his left hand, then pushed open the sliding door.

The lounge was still partially lit—there were too many track lights for any guest to find all the switches. He limped inside, listening hard (and he was the hardest of listeners). He recognized the heavy snore and labored breathing of Dr. M. He looked down the long hall and saw that the door to the master bedroom was ajar.

Matt went the other way, toward the suite's front door. Lightly tapped. The person on the other side tapped back.

Matt swung open the latch and then opened the door. A chipmunk beamed at him with white cloth teeth and huge eyes. The gigantic metal claws gripped in their hands were terrifying. "You're late," the chipmunk whispered.

"Sorry!" he whispered back.

The chipmunk leaned into the hallway, waved, and then stepped inside. They set down the claws, then removed their head like an astronaut stepping into an air lock. Kat shook out her hair. "Is he up?" she whispered.

"Asleep."

"What did you do?" She started to touch his arm with her costumed paw, then stopped herself. "You're bleeding."

"Hit the door. I'm fine."

"Okay, get out of here. You did good, Matty."

"I'll stick around—just in case." He wasn't about to make the same mistake they'd made years ago. The boys had run to the lifeboat and left her to do all the hard work. "I can get the CD out." The CD player lay on the floor, where Tusk had dropped it after he'd torn it from the wall. Matt had tried to re-trieve the CD at the end of the party, but Dr. M had spotted him and started yelling. He'd been forced to leave without it.

Kat frowned, thinking it through. "Fine. Grab it, then get back to your room." She put on the big chipmunk head, then pulled on the first claw, then the other. She'd welded them her-self backstage, two cities ago, working early in the morning when the roadies were sleeping in. It was the part of the plan that most disturbed him, but Kat had convinced him it was necessary. They needed the cops to look for a raging psycho zoomie.

"Stay out here," she said, and walked into the bedroom.

Matt stooped over the CD player. He slid his index claw into the top of the tray and pulled. The tray remained closed. He didn't have enough leverage with only one hand.

He heard a noise from the bedroom. A small, meaty noise. And then another, and another. Anyone else would have missed those noises, but not Matt.

Don't listen! he thought. Concentrate on the job!

He turned the player onto its side and gripped it between his knees. Then he worked three claws into the gap, pulled up. Something plastic snapped inside and the tray popped out, halfway. One of the CDs fell out.

Huh, he thought. Beastie Boys.

In the bedroom, Kat was moving around. He heard luggage being unzipped. Not his worry. He gritted his teeth and pulled on the tray again. The fucking CD had to be in the back slot, where the laser was.

The door to the hallway creaked open, and Matt stifled a screech of surprise.

"What is going on?" Tusk whispered. "Where's Kat?"

"She still in there," Matt said. "Help me open this."

Tusk picked up the CD player. He nodded toward the bedroom. "Is he going to hear this?"

"No," Matt said. "Maury's not going to hear anything."

"Okay." Tusk yanked, and the drawer opened with a crack. CDs spun into the air. Matt picked up one that was labeled with black Magic Marker: BARGE.

The bedroom door opened. The chipmunk stepped out, still grinning. The front fur was coated in blood. Kat stood for a long time, the claws heavy at her sides. Then she said, "I can't find the laptop." Her words were muffled by the head.

"What did you say?" Tusk said.

She lifted off the head. "I can't find the laptop. We need it."

"We're out of time," Tusk said. "The security guards can come back any moment."

"Come back?" Matt said. "When were they here?"

"Fifteen minutes ago. Bobby was making a lot of noise, and someone on the floor below complained. He just settled down, but who knows when he'll start back up."

"Fuck," Matt said.

"Fuck," Kat agreed.

"Did you check inside the computer bag?" Tusk asked. "That's where he keeps it."

"I know where he keeps it. The computer bag is empty. I went through the luggage, too, and checked under the bed, and in the closets."

"It's four ten," Tusk said. "We're behind schedule." Tusk hated to be behind schedule.

"I know, I know," Kat said. "Okay. We have to hope the police don't go through all the files. We'll get it back when they return it to Mrs. M."

When they stepped into the hallway, Matt said, "Last chance."

"Close it," Kat said.

He quietly pulled the door shut. It was good to not have to worry about fingerprints—his were pretty distinctive. Now all he had to worry about was a broken shoulder.

Tim was standing in the hallway. "Is he dead?" he asked.

"Yes, love," Kat answered.

"Good."

Kat helped Matt out of the harness. Then she said, "Shit. I forgot a pillowcase."

"I'll get one," Tim said. Kat followed him into the room.

Tusk looked at Matt. "Are we bad people?"

"We're not entirely good."

"But we had to do this, yes?"

"He would have destroyed her," Matt said. "And the baby. Just to keep us under his thumb. So I say: Fuck him."

Tusk nodded. "Indeed."

Tim and Kat emerged, Kat now holding a pillowcase full of claws in one hand and the chipmunk head in the other.

Kat pursed her lips. She looked into each of their faces. "You risked your lives for me. You risked your freedom. I can't thank you enough for that."

"You did the same for us," Tim said.

"Let's just not make a habit of this," Matt said. He was sorry that Devin and Bobby couldn't be out here, but Devin had his job keeping Mrs. M out of the way, and Bobby ... Bobby was too sweet and too naive to be trusted.

Tusk *ahem*med, and tapped his wrist.

"You're right, you're right." She pressed the elevator button.

"Matt, don't forget to get the bungee off the roof—I'll take it back to the stage in the morning and we'll pack it up."

"I know," Matt said.

"Just checking." She lifted the costume head, and paused. "You're good boys."

Tim said, "We'll be waiting for you."

"Where Do We Go from Here?"

Featuring Detective Delgado

"After she hid the costume and the claws," Luce said, "she then walked up fifty-six flights of stairs to the penthouse level, where one of you let her in." She'd been talking for ten minutes. In that time she never released her grip on her side arm. "How'd I do?"

Tusk and Matt looked at each other. Matt said, "Was there a hidden camera?" Devin put his face in his hands. Tim stared at his feet, which were encased in steel-toed work boots.

"Wait a minute," Bobby said. "You guys did all this, and you didn't tell me?!"

Kat said, "We tried to keep you out of it, love."

"Can you prove any of it?" Tusk asked Luce. He sounded genuinely curious.

"I'm afraid I can. Some of Dr. M's blood showed up where it had no business being." The blood samples from Tim's room were still in her jacket pocket. "Also, we found hair inside the chipmunk suit. Our guy thought it might be from Devin. I'm betting DNA analysis would confirm it's from Kat."

"If they got a sample from Kat to compare," Matt said.

"True," Luce said.

"How quickly did you suspect us?" Matt asked.

"From almost the beginning, this thing had the whiff of a magic act. Quick changes, scary props, drama. Plus, everyone was everyone else's alibi, which was very tidy. I had the feeling I was getting played. Then you went and mentioned Agatha Christie and John Dickson Carr, which is always suspicious."

"Argh! Dammit!"

"How soon did you suspect Kat?" Tim asked.

"The chipmunk costume really pushed me toward her," Luce told him. "Matt or Tusk couldn't fit in it, so that left you or Devin. But then I ruled out both of you—whoever wore it would have to be non-famous and be able to pass for a normal human. Sorry."

"I know what I look like," Tim said.

"And I don't take offense," Devin said.

"The point is," Luce said, "if either of you stepped out into the lobby after ditching the costume in the restroom, you'd be mobbed."

"But the killer could have just as easily have been Mrs. M," Matt said. "You always gotta suspect the spouse in a homicide."

"Oh, she was on my short list," Luce said. "She had a great motive for killing her husband, and Kat had no reason that I could see. But I couldn't shake the feeling that there was a lot to Kat's story that I didn't understand. The way you all listened to her, the baby bump she was hiding, the paramedical tattoos covering the scars . . ."

"My first introduction to Western science," Kat said, "was at the hands of a surgeon."

"Ah. I'm sorry." Luce took a breath. "Anyway, all these details made me think I was missing something. Maybe it was because I started my career as my father's assistant. Do you know how much dirty work the assistant gets away with? Nobody pays attention to the girl carrying the props on and off the stage."

"I do," Devin said. "I always appreciate and respect the roadies."

"Noted, Dev," Matt said.

"Keep going," Kat said. "You suspected me, but didn't know why, until . . ."

"Until I got Dr. M's laptop," Luce said.

"So you got past the password," Kat said. "Already."

Luce tilted her head. "I know people. I listened to the songs first. Those were recorded on the barge, right? I could hear a low background rumble. I wondered if it was the engine."

"Our captors were interested enough to record it," Kat said. Her voice had changed. The punk snarl had dropped out of it. "They thought it was amusing."

"My daughter recognized the songs," Luce said. "I hope she'll be happy someday to find out a woman wrote the music she loves. You know, Tusk admitted to me he wasn't the composer, but I thought he was being modest."

"I don't write music," Tusk said. "I remember it."

"Stop it," Kat said. "You're an amazing musician and engineer."

"So much of what you all said to me was the truth," Luce said. "What Matt told me about your genetics, what Kat told me about the PTSD you'd all experienced. When Tim got so angry defending the songs I should have realized he was defending his . . . Kat."

"You can use the word," Kat said.

"All right," Luce said. "His mother."

"Try again."

"Father?"

"Let's go with 'parent.'"

"Finally!" Bobby said. "Do we get to tell people now?"

"Still a secret, love," Kat said.

"So what do *I* call you?" Luce asked the woman. "Kat? Sofia? Subject One?"

"I doubt you could pronounce my original name," Kat said. "And I've had many since. Male names, female names, names no one could pin down. I lived free for many years, in whatever country I chose—and I could have remained free if not for a fit of misplaced altruism. I was living in England during the war, and volunteered for a project. The Americans, unfortunately, learned of my true nature. Afterward, they decided to keep me for themselves."

"Until you broke out. I'm guessing the explosion was no accident."

"They were going to terminate the boyz, there was a moment of lax security, and I seized the opportunity."

And how many people did you kill? Luce wondered. Did any of those scientists make it out alive?

"I made it off the barge well after the boyz," Kat continued. "Yet I landed in Peru well before they were rescued."

"Sure, *you* pick the lifeboat with a motor," Matt said.

Kat grimaced. "I thought they'd been recaptured, or . . . worse. Then I saw them on television and made my way to Ecuador. I decided I needed a rock and roll persona to convince Maury to take me on. I shouldn't have worried—he was desperate for help."

"And so you became Kat, Queen of the Roadies," Luce said.

"I'm a little sad to give her up—before I was her, I didn't

know the pleasure of using 'fuck' to spice up every sentence."

"It's an all-purpose condiment," Matt said. "Like Tabasco."

"You know federal agents are taking over the case," Luce said. "They're looking for someone named Jorge Heriberto."

"We're aware," Tusk said. "One of our crew spotted them in the hotel. They're not from the Fish and Wildlife Service."

"I figured."

"I've been hunted by men like them for a long time," Kat said. "I've spent too much of my life behind bars. I'll die before I go back. I won't let them have another child. How much have you read of the files Dr. M stole from us?"

"Enough to know what they did."

"They were terrified we'd breed," Kat said. "The daughters they let live a month or two. The boys they killed when they reached adolescence. And the ones in between, the ones like me? They were so afraid of them that they killed them immediately."

Luce couldn't speak. The WyldBoyZ were all looking somewhere else.

"Dr. M had copied the files from Tusk when he first met them, in Ecuador," Kat said. "Maury sat on them, not really understanding all that he had, but sensing it was valuable. He had the music producer's natural gift for blackmail."

"But he didn't know who *you* were," Luce said.

Kat nodded. "Not until a few weeks ago, when one of us slipped up, and let him know that I was on the barge, too."

"I'm *sorry*," Bobby said. "I said I was sorry!"

"It's not your fault," Kat said to him. "Maury's a predator."

"It's a little his fault," Tim said.

"Dr. M threatened to expose Kat," Luce guessed. "Turn her over to the government unless you all stayed in the band."

"She's the valuable one," Matt said. "Me and the boyz, we're locked-in, genetically. But Sofia—she's protean. Endlessly mutable."

"I don't know why I'm this way," Kat said. "Why my children are so varied and beautiful, and why I . . . keep going. Perhaps, one day, Matt will be able to explain what I am—what we all are. But I do know this. For the first time in my very long life, my children and I have the means to create a home for ourselves, a means to protect ourselves, and Dr. M threatened all of that. All of us."

"Tusk's dream," Luce said. "The remote studio where no one can bother you."

"We've pooled our money and purchased a home," Tusk said.

Kat leaned forward and locked eyes with Luce. "What you need to decide, Detective, is whether you're going to choose the simple solution, or—" Her eyes flicked to the left, past Luce's shoulder. Suddenly Kat straightened. "Hey there," she said.

Melanie stepped out of the hallway. "Mami?" Her eyes were small with sleepiness. And then, suddenly, she was wide awake.

———————

"Melanie," Luce said. "Sweetie." The girl ignored her. She stared at the people in the room, her mouth open. Luce said, "I need you to go back to bed."

Finally, Melanie looked at her mother. Her eyes were full of tears. "Is this . . . ? Is this . . . ?"

Real? thought Luce. Yeah.

"Hey now," Bobby said softly. He was sitting on the floor a few feet from Melanie. He leaned forward and bumped his head against her hand. "Don't be nervous. I'm Bobby."

"I know!" the girl wailed. "You're so soft!"

Bobby grinned. "I am, right?"

Devin came forward and extended a hand. "You must be Melanie," he said. "I'm Devin."

"Hi, Devin." She was trembling, and tears were running down her cheeks.

Tusk had gotten to his feet. "We heard you were a pretty big fan." He extended his trunk. Melanie shook it without hesitation. Matt reached out with his left wing and introduced himself. Tim slid off the chair. He was about the same height as Melanie. "I hear you write songs," he said.

"No, not like, okay, yes, but . . ."

Luce watched, her right hand tight on the gun.

Devin said, "We were leaving town, but we thought, why not stop by and sing a song with our biggest fan?"

Melanie stared at him. She wiped at her eyes. *"With?"*

"We heard you're a pretty good singer," Devin said. "Do you know this one?" He glanced up at Kat, and she sang a note: A over middle C.

"Can you see . . . it?" Devin sang. His voice was almost a whisper. He looked down at Melanie. The girl glanced back at her mother.

Luce thought, Fuck it. She nodded.

"On the horizon," Melanie sang. Her voice was shaking, but she was on key.

"Can you feel . . . it?" Devin sang.

"Our own special island," the girl sang back, stronger. Tusk and Tim and the others seemed to lean in.

"I think it might be," Devin sang. "It just might be . . ."

The WyldBoyZ sang out in mighty five-part harmony: "*Home.*"

Melanie and Devin sang the first verse together:

"*I thought I was lost, and you brought me here,*
Where the sun is warm and the water's clear."

The two kept singing, and other voices wrapped around them, braiding and blending. The WyldBoyZ were only a few feet from her, and she couldn't tell which were singing which notes.

And then, at the end of the third verse, Tim stepped between Devin and Melanie, threw out his hands, and held them there. The singing stopped.

Tusk tapped his foot, and it sounded like the pedal of a bass drum: *wump, wump, wump.*

Devin clapped his hands and called out, "Timmy says what? Timmy says what?"

"Timmy says bongos," the pangolin said.

Melanie squealed and jumped back. She knew what was coming. Devin raised his hands and then brought his palms down on Tim's armored head. Started drumming. The rhythm was fast and intricate. The ape shouted, "Bedtime, babies, bedtime!"

Everyone started chanting and hooting along with the drumming. Matt screeched high-pitched percussives, and Melanie started shouting, "He-ey! Ho! He-ey! Ho!" Luce thought, Is this from a video? How does she know how to do this?

Suddenly Timmy yelled, "Stop!" The silence hit like its own drumbeat.

Devin chanted, "Bobby says what? Bobby says what?"

Bobby jumped onto the trunk. "Bobby says dance!"

Luce stepped back, into the wall. Bobby spun around, did a James Brown split, and popped up again—all without slipping off the table.

Devin pointed at Melanie. The girl was pogoing madly, hands in the air. Devin said, "Mel says what? Mel says what?"

Melanie yelled, "Mel says *stomp*!" No hesitation.

Tusk trumpeted. Luce had never heard him do that before. He lifted one big foot and slammed it down. The house shook. He did a shimmy and stomped the other foot. Melanie clapped, madly. The glass posters rattled against the walls. Luce thought, If he breaks the house, no one will believe me.

Then she heard a voice sliding through the tweeting and stomping and drumming.

"Can you see it . . ."

It was Kat. She was standing off to the side, her head thrown back, one hand on the slight bulge of her tummy.

"Can you feel it . . ."

And someone answered: *"Home."*

"Can you see it . . ."

Another voice sang back: *"Home."*

"Can you feel it . . ."

and over and over, call and response, until, without Luce understanding how it was happening, the voices joined, became one voice, and then all of them—Kat and the WyldBoyZ and Melanie and now Luce, too, her voice emerging without her willing it—they were all singing together.

The song ended, and Melanie turned to her mother, her eyes wide in astonishment. Then she noticed what was in her mother's hand.

Luce looked down. Ah. The Glock. She said, "You need to go back to bed, Melanie."

"Mami?"

"It's all right, we've got to go," Kat said. She looked at Luce. "Are we going?"

"Melanie," Luce said. *"Now."*

Melanie had never heard that tone in her mother's voice. It shook her. She walked to the hallway, stopped. "Good night, everybody. Bobby, I'm really glad you're not in jail."

Kat said, "You're very talented, Melanie. I hope you keep singing."

"I hope you do, too," Melanie said.

Luce waited until Melanie's bedroom door closed—and was 100 percent sure her daughter was standing on the other side with her ear pressed to the door.

"That was nice of you," Luce said to the band. "But it doesn't change my decision."

They looked at her. So many strange faces.

Luce lowered her voice. "You don't get to murder someone, even if they're a terrible person. Even if they're 90 percent scumbag. We live by laws."

"'And he who breaks the law goes to the House of Pain,'" Kat said. "I've heard it before."

"You got it," Luce said. "You break the law, you get punished. That's what separates us from animals."

"Us?" Kat said.

"But the punishment has to fit the crime," Luce said. "And I won't be responsible for a genocide." She tucked the pistol behind her, into the waistband. "I sentence you to exile."

The room was quiet for a long moment. Then Bobby groaned. "Can someone pleeeease tell me what's happening?"

Kat looked at the trunk, then at Luce. "What's in there can hurt us," Kat said.

"I promised I'd return it," Luce said.

Kat reached for the latch. Luce didn't move to stop her. Kat lifted the lid—and frowned. She reached inside, knocked on the floor and sides. The trunk was empty.

"Don't worry," Luce said. "Before I give it back, I'll clean out all the bad stuff."

Kat laughed. "Fair enough."

"I still don't know what's happening," Bobby complained.

"Back to the car, love," Kat said. "It's time for *us* to vanish."

Bonus Track

P.S. I once made the mistake of telling an Englishman my story, and he turned it into a novel. And not just any novel, but a bestseller. He didn't pay me a dime. I swore to myself that next time I'd write my own story. I hope you and your mother enjoyed it.

P.P.S. Tusk asked me to add that the island has a full studio. In fact, the enclosed CD was produced entirely on-site. He would be delighted to work with you—correction, work with you again (he's such a pedant, but he has dined out for years on the fact that the WyldBoyZ were Melanie Delgado's first collaborators).

P.P.P.S. If it wouldn't be too much of a bother, my daughter Lucy would love a signed T-shirt (women's Medium). Also, my son, Bertie (men's Medium), my younger daughter, Ivy (girls Large), and my youngest, Indigo (do you sell onesies?). Oh wait, I forgot about Tusk's children, and Tim's, and Devin's (too many to count). Fuck! Just send a box and I'll distribute.

With love and admiration,
Kat

Apologies

I would first like to apologize to my children, musicians all, whom I shamefully mined for their expertise. My firstborn, Emma, brought the Backstreet Boys and NSYNC into our house when she was eight years old, when those bands were at the height of their popularity. I rolled my eyes and complained, for which I'm sorry. I think I was afraid that her obsession with bubblegum pop would stop her from appreciating the gritty authenticity of the bands of *my* youth, such as the Partridge Family and the Monkees. Instead, her music became part of the soundtrack of my life—and . . . I want it that way (tell me why).

I asked my second born, Ian Gregory, to write the first draft of Tim's impassioned defense of pop music, and they gave me the perfect rant. Third-born Mars Tozer-Whiteside helped with the Spanish. Kyle Tozer-Whiteside, fourth in line, had no idea he was helping me when he sent me videos of his band.

I would like to ask the forgiveness of my friends and fellow writers who had to listen to me talk about this silly story for a long time, and read drafts of it, especially Jack Skillingstead, Nancy Kress, Ysabeau Wilce, and Chris Farnsworth. Griffin Barber provided info on police procedures, and Erin Cashier, who is also a nurse on the COVID-19 front lines, found the poison I needed for the plot. I'm sorry if I messed up any details.

I owe Dave Justus a huge apology. This idea for this novella started with a conversation we had during a car ride between Austin and San Antonio. I say "conversation," but it was more of a ninety-minute riff session, each of us trying to crack up the other person with animal puns, the lewder the better. Dave, I'm sorry this book doesn't have more of those jokes.

I would also like to apologize to Liza Trombi, who put up with my extreme introversion while writing this during lockdown. She bought me the beautiful illustrated edition of *The Island of Dr. Moreau* with art by Bill Sienkiewicz, which I went back to time and again while writing this.

My sincere apologies to my agent, Seth Fishman, for springing this on him; to my editor, Jonathan Strahan, for refusing to change the title; and to Irene Gallo, Emily Goldman, and all the people at Tordotcom Publishing, for asking you to support such a ridiculous mashup. Your enthusiasm is baffling to me.

Finally, I would like to apologize to T. S. Eliot for breaking every one of his five rules for detective stories. I thought I might have to obey #5, and then he went and used the masculine pronoun for detectives. In the words of one of today's pop princesses, Demi Lovato, "Sorry, not sorry."

About the Author

Liza Trombi

DARYL GREGORY's most recent publication from Tor.com was the Hugo finalist novelette "Nine Last Days on Planet Earth." He's the author of six novels, including *Spoonbenders,* a Nebula, Locus, and World Fantasy Award finalist now in development at Showtime. His novella *We Are All Completely Fine* won the World Fantasy and Shirley Jackson Awards, and was a finalist for the Nebula, Sturgeon, and Locus Awards. Many of his short stories are collected in *Unpossible and Other Stories,* a *Publishers Weekly* best book of the year. Daryl lives in Oakland, California, where he recently finished a decidedly less silly novel, forthcoming from Knopf.

TOR·COM

Science fiction. Fantasy. The universe.

And related subjects.

*

More than just a publisher's website, *Tor.com*
is a venue for **original fiction, comics,** and
discussion of the entire field of SF and fantasy,
in all media and from all sources. Visit our site
today—and join the conversation yourself.